Ghosts

who

Google

Selected stories
by

Stephen Atkinson

Circaidy Gregory Press

Copyright information

paperback ISBN 978-1-906451-81-3
First published May 2013
ebook ISBN 978-1-906451-60-8
First published May 2013

Printed in the UK by
MPG Books Group

Published by Circaidy Gregory Press
Creative Media Centre,
45 Robertson St, Hastings,
Sussex TN34 1HL

www.circaidygregory.co.uk

About the Author

Stephen Atkinson has been a lifelong journalist for one primary reason; his fierce passion for writing. But when at sixteen he fled the suburban family home for the Big City, 'being a writer' was never going to pay London bed-sit rents. Newspapers and magazines beckoned as an obvious second best despite an irritating obsession with obstacles known as 'facts'. Now in retirement he writes purely for pleasure, strums a guitar and hooks the occasional mackerel from an old fishing boat on the Sussex coast.

Scavenger first appeared in *Barcelona to Bihar,* published by Earlyworks Press. Stephen also had two stories printed in a previous Earlyworks Press anthology, *Ways of Falling*. They were *Five Little Pinkies* and *Rabbit Punch.* All were shortlisted entries in the international short story competition. His short science fiction story, *A Life to Die For*, won a prize and was published in Writers' Forum in October 2012 and a humorous short, *Mr Braithwaite Contends*, appeared in Stringybark Publishing's *The Seven Deadly Sins* anthology in Australia in 2012. He has won various other prizes in literary competitions. Most recently, his stories *I've Had a Terrible Day* and *Lady Keep Your Hat On*, were highly commended and selected for publication this year in an Australian Humorous Writing contest and *The Last Bullet*, to be published in an Earlyworks Press collection in 2013. He says he has been short-listed, long-listed, black-listed and ham-fisted more times than he cares to remember.

Acknowledgements

Sincerest thanks to Jan Sampson for all her love, patience and encouragement, not to mention her superb artwork on the front and back cover. Also to the spookiest trio of them all Amy, Emily and Michael. And to lay a lingering ghost, a special mention for K.T.

Foreword

As far as I know, I've never had the honour of meeting a ghost but I believe it to be a foolish mistake to deny their existence. In our modern age of quantum physics we live with the inexplicable every single day, without even knowing it. Bewildered scientists are learning that the mysterious antics of neutrons, photons and protons forming the very basis of existence are as spooky as anything we can dream up. Perhaps they could even explain some of the strange phenomena related in this book...

Stephen Atkinson March 2013

Contents

Scavenger

He worries her in a way she can't entirely understand, riffling through a small litterbin bracketed four feet up the pole of an old-fashioned gas lamp. A yellowish glow massages his etched features, his aquiline nose, strange high forehead and dirt encrusted cheekbones. She stares but pretends not to at his wild, caked eyebrows and realises with disgust she is disgusted.

Just some old tramp, down on his luck and hoping to find a faintly warm discarded burger and maybe a day old greasy Guardian to read as he dines. One of life's unfortunates; no threat to her.

Still, behind a charade of reaching for a cigarette, she deftly transfers the Mace in her handbag to her raincoat pocket and fingers it there, savouring its reassurance.

She waits here by the river because this is where she always waits. It is their secret place and they know they can entrust themselves to its dark, seldom trod Victorian passages. She can see the moon shimmering faintly on the water, yielding just enough light to render the cranes and warehouses a menace of their own. He is late and she finds herself a little afraid.

Suddenly she is aware the down-and-out is looking straight at her, a battered punnet of what was once strawberries or maybe cherries clutched in his half-mitted right hand. His smile is not aggressive or impolite; just unsettlingly weird.

In her head she rehearses appropriate responses to anything inappropriate he may be about to grunt at her.

Good evening – I hope I'm not disturbing you, is all she can think of to say. She stays silent.

He stares but says nothing. The blackened, time-polished brickwork at his back affords him a Dickensian appearance. His long shabby overcoat has but one button left, the rest a mere memory. She thinks of Fagin. All he lacks is the tall, crumpled hat.

"I have three questions for you." She jumps at the sound of his voice, mannered, educated even, but peculiarly unnatural.

She is shocked into silence. God, where is he? Why is he always late?

"Should a Matisse hang in your library, why covet a Vermeer?"

She is too stunned to think. *What the hell is he talking about? I have no Matisse. No library either.*

His silence mates with hers, an intimate empty void.

"I thought...I thought you said three questions," she stutters.

"The remaining two are for you to ask," he replies, voice soft with commanding confidence. Those eyes that had seemed to her in the London dark dead and vacant, now seem to gently mock.

"I don't understand." She can think of nothing but an ardent prayer for footsteps to ring on the backstreet cobbles.

"Few of us do." The tramp looks away briefly at the polystyrene punnet in his right hand, sniffs derisively, and flings it back in the bin from whence it came. He turns and without another word disappears under the railway arch.

She is left gasping for breath in fear and relief. From the opposite direction she hears the sound she has been waiting for.

"Robin!" breathes Lucy Brewster's voice, but her heart is really screaming for her father.

Jim Brewster waits for the gull to finish pecking at the fish on the low roof before advancing further towards his cockleshell home. A flurry of wings as an interloper swoops in for his share and both birds take to the sky screeching, the titbit firmly in the yellow beak of the thief and the other in hot pursuit.

Only now does he crouch below the low lintel and enter his makeshift beach shack. Inside it is dark, lit by candle and paraffin only at night, and even his eagle eyes struggle to locate what he is looking for. After a moment he takes a large can from a shelf and returns to the bright sunlight outside.

He takes the can to a rock-pool some 20 yards across the sand and feeds the contents into a thin-necked, green bottle strapped beneath the waterline with twine. This trap for the graceful but stupid Ba'la bird provides him with a good percentage of his monthly sustenance. The egret-like scavenger can't resist the smell of powdered coffee, but – just like the monkey who traps his hand in a rock cleft because he doesn't have the sense to unclench his fistful of nuts – the Ba'la gets his dumb head lodged in the neck of the bottle and can't escape. His muffled cries for help at twilight are an eerie alert that game is on the table.

Jim tests the semi-submerged trap for sturdiness and then follows his barefoot prints in the sand back to the shack. He replaces the coffee and then steps outside again to check the haphazard timber crossbeams. The hut is made entirely from flotsam scavenged from his lonely, white sand shores and decorated with large and small seashells of every colour. White baked clay walls keep out the sun but are no match for the local monsoon rains. When the wet season comes, he might just as well sleep out under a palm frond for all the shelter his hut affords.

The rain is not cold and unpleasant as in his native Essex and it's simply a case of waiting for the sun to come up with the dawn, and then to dry out literally in seconds.

Jim is the only man on the island and that's the way he likes it. Further into the Solomons many more are inhabited and occasionally he gets visitors, some welcome, some not. With a good stash of cash and barter goods, he relies heavily on this occasional outrigger trade.

Natives who canoed by chance from 50 miles away once saved him from a fever and he could never forget that. With not a word of common tongue they nursed him for three days and three nights. He knew he could have died but for their timely appearance.

He has no contact with the outside world. No radio. No phone. No boat.

He strokes his white, scruffy beard as his other hand presses a conch shell further into the soft clay wall. High winds sometimes take exception to his sense of the aesthetic.

A soft squeaking alerts him to two sea otters surveying him from a safe distance, unsure of their welcome. They come almost every day, hoping for a snack he may lay out for them if he's feeling generous. In truth, he mostly appreciates their company; playful and carefree, their antics on the sand remind him of watching Lucy and Ben when they were young, building sandcastles at Walton-on-the-Naze.

"Come on then, my furry friends," he entreats, placing some small morsels on their usual feeding stone.

He watches for a moment as they warily creep towards their own Hard Rock Cafe, knowing their shyness will disappear as soon as they know he's in a giving mood. He isn't always.

They tuck in and he is free to rise and fetch a battered, cardboard box from inside the shack. Intent on their feast, they don't even flinch when he ducks his head in and then out again.

He sits on his own rock, next to the dormant cook fire, and relaxes with his memories. He takes out first one photo and then another, placing them down carefully beside him.

Many of the pictures are of Lucy; Lucy in the garden at Theydon Bois; Lucy at High Beech in Epping Forest; Lucy on the sands at Clacton or Old Leigh.

There are also of course pictures of Lucy's mother and of Ben, but he spends less time looking at those. Ben took his mother's side in the brutal collapse of his marriage. There is a picture of Ben smiling broadly after catching a monster sea bass on a week's sea fishing holiday with his mother and her new boyfriend Roger. Roger and Ben hit it off just fine.

Ben had his own life and was free to go the way he chose and Jim didn't celebrate the feeling of betrayal he felt deep inside. He tried to fight it, but it lingered there like a cancer.

Jim came to the island to forget – to forget everything, his marriage, his job as head of the Institute Research Lab, everything.

But the one thing he couldn't quite forget was Lucy. She was still vulnerable and extremely liable to make treacherous mistakes. Mistakes like Robin for instance.

Before he decided to throw it all up and bury himself in cocooned isolation she had made no secret of her affair with a married man. It was a sad scene alright, but it was her choice.

Jim looked up as the squealing otters started to fight. The food had gone and they were bored. But it was just playful jousting. Unlike Robin. Jim strongly suspected that Robin was not quite the gentleman he pretended to be. Once Lucy had phoned him at the flat, crying. She wouldn't talk then but when they met later at London Bridge she was wearing dark glasses and refused to take them off. It was night.

When Jim later told her he was throwing up everything to live like a hermit on some remote island she had stared at him in astonishment.

"Why?" she had asked, simply.

He didn't know why, he told her. He just was.

She seemed to understand his need to run away from the ugly ruins of his derelict marriage – even running away from the institute. It was a high-powered job, but demanding and she knew it drained him.

"Your book?" she asked. "You'll still write your book?"

"Maybe," he'd replied. He'd been planning the book for years and she loved it when he talked about it. She could share his excitement, his enthusiasm. She knew that when everything else was falling apart around him, his book was still his dream.

But the truth was, he didn't even bring a typewriter to the island. He chartered a one-way ticket with a native fisherman and took little with him to tie him to his old life.

The photos were an exception.

He sits musing for hours and stirs only as the heat begins to lose its intensity. He looks up to find the otters gone and the sun beginning to dip to the distant horizon.

Shaking himself from his lethargy, he rises to take the cardboard box of memories back inside. He goes with a heavy heart – he isn't proud of the fact that he has given up everything, he just has. Now, as so many times before, he feels the heavy burden of guilt; guilt that he hasn't the guts to face up to real life anymore, and guilt for not standing his ground to protect Lucy.

He steps in the hut – and stops stock still. Even in the dim light he can see the shape of something that just can't be there; the shape of a man.

"What the hell..?"

A cold shiver travels down his spine and up again, settling uncomfortably in the back of his head.

For this is no loin-clothed, native wanderer. This man is fully dressed - in a damned overcoat, no less.

"Who the hell are you?" Jim demands again, his heart pounding. Nobody has stepped on the island for three months and this figure is bizarre in the extreme.

"Answer me!"

The figure in the gloom turns to him but oddly Jim doesn't feel threatened. He struggles to conjure details for clues and sees something straight out of the pages of a book on Dickensian London.

“I have two questions for you,” says a voice, quiet, patient and well mannered.

Jim is struck dumb.

“Whatever would the English discuss if they suffered a less volatile climate than their own?”

Jim’s head is filled with the absurd picture of two men in bowler hats meeting in the Sahara.

Morning, Brown. Turned out sunny again!

He waits for the intruder to continue, but no sound comes.

“You said two questions,” he prompts.

“The other is for you to ask.”

At that the figure brushes past him and stoops to negotiate the door. Jim can feel his rough tweed coat against his bare skin as he goes, and is aware of a vague smell of damp and tobacco.

He follows him out into the dying evening sunshine.

“Ask what? Ask whom?” he persists but can only stand and gape as the strange figure ambles across the beach to the water’s edge. With a dismissive grunt he carelessly tosses aside a pretty pink shell he has taken from a shelf inside the hut and keeps walking until his head disappears under the foamy sea.

Jim manages to get his muscles to obey him at last and tears across the sand to dive headlong into the waves.

But search as he might, he can find no trace of his mystery visitor. Baffled, he stands waist high in the ocean even as the island’s brief twilight turns to sudden and almost complete dark.

It is not true to say that Ben didn’t struggle with his conscience when he was asked to take over his father’s post at the institute. He struggled, but not for long. A six-figure salary is very persuasive.

After all, at 34 he was the perfect candidate. He had his father’s brain and had worked alongside him for twelve years, since leaving Oxford. He had taken the inside track and impressed the Faculty with his drive and competence.

But now the new head was deeply embroiled in a battle of conscience his father never had to face.

“You want me to sanction an experiment that might potentially put thousands and thousands of lives at risk?” His question has been posed many times before in the last hour. This is its latest metamorphosis.

The Director of Field Studies and Research had flown over from Singapore for this meeting and isn't about to be fazed by a younger version of his quitter Dad. He remains calm and patient.

"The consensus is zero risk. The region is sparsely populated at worst, totally devoid of human population at best." Richard Jenkins folds the sheaf of papers on the desk in front of him for the umpteenth time. Thrice in quick succession he bangs their lower edge gently against the highly polished wood.

He is punctuating his point. Ben hears only a warning drumbeat.

"We've searched and there is nowhere else in the world we can carry out this controlled experiment," chimes in Field Executive Charles Davidson.

"If successful, benefits to international fishing industries will be phenomenal. Think of it – a natural chemical booster that is estimated to accelerate fish breeding by two hundred per cent..."

"The seas will be literally teeming – seas that have hitherto witnessed grossly depleted fish stocks." That was Sir David Wheeler, on the board and a Government high roller.

"Isn't 'natural chemical booster' something of a contradiction?" Ben knows he is fighting a losing battle. The board knows it too.

This thing can go ahead with or without him. He has seen the hushed-up report from enfeebled American agents warning of a minimal risk. The financial stakes are high – but one drawing board error could spell ecological disaster for the Solomon Islands with everything poisoned in its seas for thousands of square miles.

But, pound for pound, a six-figure salary carries more weight than a lorry-load of integrity.

"I'll sleep on it," says Ben sharply. Some of the key players in the room exchange impatient glances.

"A unanimous go-ahead is imperative now," says Jenkins softly. "We have the whole operation on hold this instant. Two dozen ships on standby, helicopters...the works."

Ben thinks of his absent father, eking a pathetic existence by fishing in the blue coral seas somewhere near the Solomons. He could find no respect in his heart for him. Roger was right – his dad was a pathetic quitter. He'd abandoned them, his job and even his book… *Who knows, maybe I can increase your red snapper catch two hundred fold. Cast that line, Dad – gonna be rainin' fish!*

"Ok. I just need a bathroom break. Give me five and then I think we can safely say we're in business."

Ben can feel the relief around the table and Jenkins allows himself a tight smile as he removes the top sheet of his sheaf of papers and places it face up in front of him, a Mont Blanc pen positioned expectantly across the page.

Ben strides purposefully to the bathroom through a door off to the right. It is a sumptuous pee palace, with marble walls, piped Debussy and gold ribboned soaps at every basin.

He stares at his face in the mirror, stretching the muscles around his eyes, nose and mouth to exorcise the weariness he feels.

He starts as behind him he is aware of a figure. A strange hobo in a long scruffy overcoat with most of the buttons missing.

Ben wheels around. "Who the blazes...?"

"I have two questions to ask." Ben pulls back from the unpleasant stench that this man exudes, a reflex action that he at once regrets.

"Ah, you find my aroma unpleasant," observes the stranger.

"If we are considering bad smells, let me ask you this. Would Jesus resort to Strontium 90 to share his five fish among the 5,000?"

"How the...?" Ben is stunned, not just by the question but by the peculiar timbre of the man's voice. Even in this echoing bathroom, it doesn't sound right.

"You said two questions!"

"The other only you can pose."

Ben's attention is distracted by the opening of the bathroom door.

"They're wondering if you're OK," says Taylor, a minion. "You've been some time."

"I..." Ben turns to the hobo, but he has gone.

"I'm coming." He turns to rinse his hands under the gold plated tap before he follows Taylor back into the conference room. The last thing he notices is that the gold ribboned soap has vanished.

"Are we all decided then?" asks Jenkins, eagerly proffering the document awaiting Ben's final signature.

Ben stands before them a moment, totally silent.

"I have a question," he says. The room is hushed, expectant.

"When I blow this whole gaffe to the international Press in a moment or two, how long do you think it will be before your whole damnable project disintegrates before your very eyes?"

Robin takes Lucy into his arms just as a light drizzle begins to glisten the cobbles beneath their feet.

"Sorry I'm late. The wife..." His face is contorted with contrite pain.

She pulls away from the warmth of the blue corduroy jacket she has always found so comforting.

"I have a couple of questions to ask you," she says quietly. He looks curious, but unafraid.

"If you have a Matisse hanging in your library, why covet a Vermeer?"

"Are you comparing Beth with a Matisse? And yourself with a Vermeer?" He is smug and amused. "What's your other question?"

"How does this compare to a punch in the face?"

"How does what…?" But his question remains unasked in a blinding flash of pain as Lucy squirts him straight in the eyes with the Mace.

He collapses screaming onto the cobblestones, his face in his hands, and Lucy strides off towards the nearest Tube.

On a tiny South Pacific island Jim Brewster is gathering as many notebooks and scraps of paper as he can find.

He checks that the stub of his pencil is good for a head start on 80,000 words and licks the end of it, thoughtfully. He scribbles...

SCAVENGER

The scavenging Ba'la bird sees nothing but the ground about his feet, and finally finds his head trapped in the neck of a tight, green bottle where he can scream no questions and hear no answers.

Hubble Bubble

Double double, toil and trouble;
Fire burn, cauldron bubble
– Macbeth Act 4 Scene 1

A corridor. White. Pristine white like the nurses' uniforms invading my space in that narrow, carpet-tiled highway, suffocating me with smiles that tell me I'm Fine. I'm not fine. The fleeting smiles lie. And neither do I trust the signs on the doors I shuffle past. Paediatrician... Travel Nurse... Dr Brown... WC – Too late to hide there. Perhaps sanctuary later, when the dreaded sample is required. A door opens and in the gap shines a neon smirk, luring me into a den of cold stethoscopes and hot poultices, a Pandora's Box of false promise.

"Mr Bailey. Come in. Come in."

I slide in sideways, not wanting to be here. It is enemy territory and is well charted. Here Be Dragons but no treasure. Nothing for me but prescriptions, predictions, dire diagnoses, and prior prognoses. Barn sized grins and soccer pitch conjecture. No cure, no fee, just the devil to pay. Abandon Hope All Ye Who Enter Here.

"How are we today, Mr Bailey? Splendid, splendid. Sit down. Relax."

I can't relax. I am dying. You can't relax when you're dying. It's like premature surrender. Dying souls don't relax. They relax when they're dead.

"Let me see, now." He peers over his glasses at notes on a screen. "We last saw you... three weeks ago." He says it like an accusation. He tries to hide it but the charge is laid. I say nothing. I wait for the dreadful moments to pass. "You can't have used up all your medication."

Commendations on the wall. Words and signatures drawn with extravagant, flowing sigils testify to degrees of competence. Two grand certificates endorsed by the hand of eminent medics flank a strange but familiar picture. It is a small boy in a dark wood. I want to be that small boy. I run through the trees and hide in the deep gloom. Only I can't run any more. I can barely walk. There is a rotting wood gate, partly closed. That's me, a rotting, partly closed gate.

"How is the... pain?" He says it like he doesn't believe there is any, like I don't lay awake almost every night trying to fight the fires that consume the dreaming. Still I say nothing. I don't have to say anything. We are bitter enemies, this doctor and I. It is a game. I crawl in on my hands and knees to beg for succour, knowing there is nothing in the medicine cabinet but platitudes and placebos.

"You *are* taking your medicine, Mr Bailey? Good, good. We want to be a good patient, now don't we?"

No, we don't want to be a good patient. We want to be a well patient. I have been coming here for months and the pain comes in with me and limps out the door with me, grimacing, when I go. I want to dump it in an untidy little pile on his tidy little desk. I want to stride out with a smile, not with more prescriptions for medicines that don't work. But I can never leave it behind. It hangs in me somewhere like ballast, ugly and heavy.

It is the usual story. I don't know why I tell her I'll come. She packs me off with a shopping list and a stern reminder to remember my appointment. But I walk in and walk out, the same diseased wreck. I'm not listening, but I know it's over. I'm leaving, his hand on my shoulder. His smile bigger than his face, he ushers me out with demonic courtesy.

"Come back if the pain gets worse. Keep taking the pills." *Shut up and go home and die quietly.*

After the tests and the heart-freezing result, I positively drowned in a sea of concerned, sad faces. Briefly. Then follows the awful counselling that Irene was encouraged to attend, sitting beside me to offer up a constant soundtrack of whimpers and soft sobs.

"You must remain positive at all times," the counsellor says. "Pursue those things that most interest you. Involve yourself in projects you have always flirted with." He pauses, possibly editing his own flirtations. "Hang-gliding perhaps, or write a novel or learn a musical instrument. This need not be a lonely path. You are surrounded by people who care."

More whimpers and soft sobs. Between them, Irene manages to blurt out the question I dare not entertain.

"How... long?"

"Perhaps a year. The doctors aren't specific."

"Perhaps...?" I venture hesitantly, not really wanting to know.

"Perhaps less."

Irene's whimpers and sobs rise to a perfect cadence.

Back in the white corridor. Past the Paediatrician... the Travel Nurse... Dr Brown. I didn't even get to the cool WC sanctuary, with its plug-in fragrance. My mind is in a confused whirl as usual. I am a human being – just – but going through the motions. Whatever is expected of me I try to present, acquiescence in action. *Keep taking the pills. We want to be a good patient, now don't we?*

The doctors show intense interest at first. I am flattered. I am a fascinating item. Not every day does a humdrum GP come across an incurable case. I am passed from pillar to post, from hospital to hospital, from specialist to specialist. I am *special.* For a while. But even medical enigmas have a sell-by date, and when they've exhausted their latest revolutionary miracle medicines I become just another bit of human flotsam washed up on the beach. The incurable remains uncured.

"Mr Bailey. Step inside please."

A door I had never noticed. No nameplate, just a space where one once had been. A shuffling man in old-fashioned tweed, stethoscope around his neck. Unrecognised, but giving off a strange mixed aroma of pipe tobacco and... what? Soft earth, that's it. Newly turned soil. He is already leaning over a desk, scribbling. He turns and thrusts something at me. A piece of paper; another prescription, another study in penned paralysis.

"Try this."

"I'm with Dr… er... Sutcliffe. I've just seen him."

A conspiratorial finger lifts to his lips. He has honest eyes, as befits a doctor in tweeds who smells of pipe tobacco and who favours gardening as a pastime. What a luxury, to have faith in a future in which to invest your time with fork and trowel, to watch things flourish and grow at their own leisurely pace.

"Shhhh!"

I take the piece of paper and slip it into my pocket, gratified to have at least something to take to the pharmacy across the road. No matter how cynical we become, the spectre of hope needs only the tiniest nudge.

But I hadn't anticipated the reaction I would get from the chemist.

"Is this some sort of joke?" He is staring at the prescription I had proffered. He looks at me and then leans down to whisper something in the ear of his young assistant, a girl. She too glances my way and then retires to the back of the shop, away from the counter. I strain to see. She is clutching a telephone.

"Take a seat, Mr Bailey. This won't take a moment."

I do as I am told, unable to muster the energy to enquire what might be wrong. Moments later a woman I recognise as the surgery Travel Nurse bustles in and heads straight for me. She feels my brow and takes my pulse. She is businesslike, but anxious. "Are you feeling alright, Mr Bailey? I've just seen you in the surgery, haven't I?"

I nod.

"Did you see Dr Wilson?"

"Sutcliffe."

"Did he give you a prescription?" I stay silent.

"Did Dr Sutcliffe give you a prescription for more medication?" She is insistent.

"What's wrong with the prescription?" I ask, dodging the question. I stand and try to approach the counter. I feel dizzy and the room sways. I am aware, gratefully, of the nurse's arm around my shoulders. She is a sturdy woman. The chemist is glaring at me, his face a contradictory collage, both suspicious and concerned. He doesn't know what to think.

"First of all I've never heard of Dr Bennett," he announces as calmly as he can, concealing an avalanche of anger. "And this prescription appears to be more than 50 years out of date."

He is waving it about under my nose for emphasis and I make a grab for it.

"Let me see that." My sudden movement takes the nurse unawares and she stumbles, unable to stop me.

"Mr Bailey. Please calm down," she implores.

I collapse back in my seat in disbelief, scanning the detailed instructions in longhand to mix a cocktail of medicines for Mr A. Bailey. It is signed by Dr Bennett and dated June 3rd, 1957.

"If it's some sort of practical joke, Mr Bailey..." The pharmacist's accusatory tone is cut short by the nurse's withering look. A few minutes later she has checked by telephone with Dr Sutcliffe who presumably confirmed he hadn't prescribed anything for me on this visit.

Her hushed conversation with the pharmacist drifts to my ears in snatches as I slump in a kind of stupor, aware of the pitying gaze of several other patients queuing for their medicine.

"...incurable... great strain... can't come to terms..."

They come to me, the nurse and the chemist, cautiously, as if approaching a leper. The chemist looks down at me, almost fatherly.

"You'll understand that I can't make up this prescription for you, even if I wanted to." Then to the nurse he adds: "A lot of this is actually available over the counter, without prescription. The strange thing is, some of the ingredients have changed names over half a century. I wouldn't have thought Mr Bailey would have been aware of that..."

Again he is hushed by the nurse's deep frown. She remains more mindful of my feelings and my mental state.

"You know, I think I have heard of a Dr Bennett," she says. "I'll check at the surgery to see if it rings any bells with anyone."

The chemist holds out a grasping palm to me. "Perhaps I should take the..."

Petulantly I shove the crumpled paper at him and bolt for the door. Worried protests fill the room as I leave, hurrying home knowing that I won't breathe a word to Irene about any of this.

When he unclenched his fist, the pharmacist may have believed that 4lbs of potatoes, a French stick, St Agur cheese and a bottle of Stone's Ginger Wine were Dr Bennett's answer to all my troubles.

It was Irene's shopping list. I still had the prescription.

It didn't take much research to discover that there *had* been a Dr Bennett at the surgery in the 40s and 50s. Under a pretext, I even found the door with no name-plate, now a cluttered storeroom with a musty smell not a million miles from pipe tobacco. He hanged himself in 1957 after the BMA's General Medical Council ordered him struck off for 'dangerous and illicit conduct' said to have risked the deaths of several elderly patients. Nevertheless, he was popular, a friendly, pipe-smoking individual very proud of his prize-winning blooms.

But he stood accused by the BMA of 'cavalier, irresponsible and risky' experiments with medicines, particularly in regard to desperate, hopeless cases.

That was me to a T.

With the help of the internet it was easy, finding the ingredients he had listed – even when some of them were now known by different terms. Some may not even have been strictly legal, but I became quite an expert as I scoured chemists and the web.

Hubble Bubble... Shakespeare's dark and widely misquoted couplet took on a lighter tone as I dabbled like one of Macbeth's three witches with a pinch of this and a dash of that. Step by step I pieced together the medication the late Dr Bennett had somehow prescribed for me.

Cavalier, irresponsible and risky it might have been – but that was five years ago and I'm still here and the pain very much isn't.

To Irene's delight, I've even put my name down for an allotment. *What a luxury, to have faith in a future in which to invest your time with fork and trowel, to watch things flourish and grow at their own leisurely pace.*

Sadly, in the event, Dr Bennett was unable to take advantage of that God-given luxury. But, thanks to his ministrations from beyond the grave, I am, and grateful that even as a ghost, he never forgot he was a doctor.

A Question of Suitability

The pub bench outside *The Rose and Crown* was a little rickety and wobbled each time they reached for their drinks, a pint of Harvey's and a snowball. The evening was cool and clear, a blessed relief from the claustrophobic high-summer heat earlier that day. Jason looked at her solemnly.

"Are you even listening to me?"

Tanya smiled, but it was little more than a flicker, hardly enough to disturb any feature of the pretty face Jason loved so desperately.

"Yes, of course. You said we should start married life in a new flat." She took a hasty sip of her snowball, a trifle distracted, removed the cocktail stick and popped the morello cherry into her mouth.

He stared longingly at her lips, and glared with jealousy at an inanimate object which until a few minutes ago had spent much of its existence marinating in a glass jar. If he'd raised his eyes to hers, where his gaze normally obsessed, he might have noticed something a little furtive about her baby blues which, for an instant, seemed to be less interested in him than in the unlit window of the Boots chemist further up the street.

"Yeah," he said. "It'll cost, but far better to start off in a home of our own mutual cherry...er, choosing."

Tanya nodded, lowering her eyes to her straw. She had definitely seen *him*, just for a split second, darting from the Boots alley to the darkened doorway of the British Legion. Surreptitiously she peered over her drink and into the gloomy recess, 100 yards away, but could see nothing. Wait...a faint hint of movement, a white shirt sleeve. Damn, it was definitely him. She shuddered.

"Are you OK?" Jason put his arm around her. He never needed much of an excuse. "Darling, you *are* happy, aren't you?"

She turned then to offer him her straightest, most honest expression and almost died of shame at the concern in his eyes.

"Yes, of course," she said again. "I really, really couldn't be happier. We'll choose a lovely home outside town, with a view of fields and the forest. It will be wonderful." She put down her drink so she could take both his hands in hers. She squeezed them firmly, a physical demonstration of sincerity.

It was enough to wash the doubts from his creased brow. His smile made a welcome return.

"I really do love you," he said, totally smitten.

"And I you – with all my heart."

The next day they shopped at Asda's. It was to be their first romantic meal together since the Big Party so it had to be special. He wanted salmon because she preferred fish but she insisted on his favourite, steak, served rare and simply embellished with new potatoes and spinach. There would be no eggs and definitely no chips. She would see they began their new lives together as she meant them to carry on – with a healthy diet. No more greasy spoon fry-ups, which she had suffered just to please him, and certainly no more burgers, KFC or Indian takeaways. Well, maybe sometimes.

Jason was perusing the shelves with renewed domestic interest. He was never much for shopping, but this expedition held fresh excitement for him. They were now cooking as a couple, engaged and engaging.

"Curried beans?" he ventured, taking a small can from a high shelf and making a show of reading the ingredients with intense interest. He immediately replaced it at her disapproving wince. "Humph!"

Tanya grinned and took his hand in hers before placing it on the shopping trolley for him to push. She scampered off to another aisle.

"Look!" she called excitedly. "Natural yoghurt and goat's cheese." Jason pulled a face and she came back to him, laughing. "Having doubts darling?"

"Perhaps," he teased. "Or I may just eat out a lot."

He abandoned guardianship of the trolley to take her in his arms and so failed to see the sinister change in her expression. Her face, half buried in his shoulder, suddenly darkened as she caught sight of something at the end of the canned goods section. *For God's sake – leave me ALONE*, her insides screamed silently. Although just a lightning glimpse, she knew it was *him.* There was no mistaking that trademark limp and that creased white shirt. Red memories whipped, disentangled, and then whipped again.

After a rather edgy meal at Tanya's one-room bedsit overlooking the park, Jason had gone home in something of a huff to get a good night's sleep alone. She sat on her sofa, dreamily finishing the glass of Pinot Grigio in her hand. Yes, she loved him, she knew, but for how long could she endure this farce? How long could she go on pretending nothing was wrong? She held the cool glass to her forehead and tried to let the mellow, soft jazz wash away her troubles. Her place was a mess, the bed dishevelled and accusing, but she couldn't be bothered to straighten up tonight. She too had to be bright and eager for work in the morning. She put down her empty glass and sighed a deep, resigned sigh. But before she could turn in she was disturbed by a soft rapping at her window. He'd probably come back to make up, she thought. Maybe she should clear the air and tell him exactly what's going on.

When she opened the door her heart crumpled to the same messy state as her room. "It's you." She went icy cold with a mixture of fear and loathing. She turned disgustedly back into the room leaving the door ajar. Nevertheless, she did not skip the civilities. "Tea?"

"Don't be silly."

"Sorry. I forgot." She turned to face him, summoning urgency to her voice and expression. "Dad, I'm not fourteen any more. You've got to let me lead my own life."

"You'll always be fourteen to me, you know that. I just don't think you should rush into anything. Are you sure he's the one for you?"

"Dad!" She slapped a pile of magazines she was absent-mindedly tidying back down on the coffee table with an angry *whuump.* "I can't have you spying on me all the time. It's embarrassing and, frankly, a little sick."

"I'm not spying. I'm... I'm..."

"*Spying!* And very badly – I can't look up without spotting you lurking around some corner like James Bond. I feel like a prisoner."

"I'm sorry. I try to be discreet. But since the accident… you know... my limp... I'm not as agile as I was."

Her face wore a pained look that was exclusively reserved for her father. "That's not the point, Dad. You've just got to leave me alone. I'm a big girl now and I'm engaged and Jason and I want to live our lives in peace without you snooping on us all the time."

"It's only because I care about you. I just think you could have done better for yourself than some... some second hand car salesman."

"I know that, Dad. But I'm grown up now and things have moved on. You've got to let us be. Anyway, he's not a second hand car salesman. He sells brand new saloons from a posh showroom on the High Street."

Her father shrugged and turned away to sulk. She gazed, both disapproving and sad, at his rumpled, grubby shirt and the rather odd stoop he had now adopted. Beyond the fear, there was still compassion.

"Come on Dad. We've all got to move on. Please stop monitoring our every movement. Jason's a nice guy – you'd love him, I promise. I've really got to get some sleep now."

She turned to the kitchenette to fix herself some tea and glanced back when she'd filled the kettle. But she was staring at an empty room – he had gone. With a shrug, she strode across to close the still open door, returned to switch off the kettle and fell into bed, exhausted.

The next day Jason phoned her at the hairdressing salon, his voice high with excitement.

"Jason, I've asked you not to call me at work."

"But honey I've got important news – I've been promoted. More money – so we can afford to be a little more ambitious, flat hunting. How about that? Terry said I'd done so well he wanted to make me Chief Salesman."

"That's fabulous news, darling. We'll talk about it tonight; your place. See you then. Goodbye. "

She replaced the receiver and mumbled an apology to her boss Stephanie. "He's been promoted. Couldn't wait to tell me."

"That's alright, Tanya. That's nice. Just at the right time with your engagement and everything. Promotion means more readies, vital when you are just starting out together. When's the wedding?"

"Oh, we haven't decided that yet. There's no hurry, we..." But Stephanie was no longer listening, and anyway probably couldn't hear her over the howl of the hair dryer.

That evening Jason was like an over-excited schoolboy as he discussed exactly how much extra cash his new job would put in the kitty.

"'Course, Terry says I'll have to have a new car. Can't have his top salesman running around in an old jalopy, can he? But he says he'll get me a good deal with the best company discount he can wrangle."

"Sounds expensive," mused Tanya, her brow furrowed.

"It'll be fine. We'll easily manage on my new salary. We're heading up, up and *awaaaaay*!"

Tanya didn't want to spoil his mood, he was so happy. But she didn't feel she could keep her secret from him any longer. She had to bring this farce out in the open.

"Jason."

"Yes?"

"I've something to tell you."

"Oh dear." He slumped down on his leather swivel chair. "This sounds ominous. Is it your mother again?"

"No, not this time. It's my father. I'm afraid he really doesn't want us to get married. He keeps snooping on me... on us. He just won't leave me alone."

"Your father? I thought he died in that awful car crash when you were fourteen?"

"Yes, he did."

Ne'er Even a Whisper

It was entirely typical of Trish. Sometimes she'd come early and sometimes she'd come late, just as he was settling down to sleep. Once she'd even come just before lunchtime, in broad daylight, as he was whisking up two eggs for an omelette, but he wasn't exactly sure about that. He always excused her tardiness though, as it was quite a miracle that she came at all. After all, she'd been dead five years.

The first time was about four years after she was killed in that absurd accident at the shopping centre, right outside Woolworths. She was standing at the bus stop when a man on a moped pulled up to ask directions. Just as he lifted his visor, a flatbed truck caught his rear wheel with such force that both he and Trish were sent sprawling through Woollie's plate glass window. The moped man survived, protected in heavy riding clothes and somewhat cushioned by Trish whose light summer dress was easily pierced by lethal shards of broken glass, more than one of which penetrated her long, slender back to lodge in a vital organ. Trish died instantly.

Raymond rarely talked about the accident, but not for the reasons most people suspected. The fact was, it was so bizarre that when he explained it, it was as if he was telling some sort of funny story and was afraid that at some point he would smile, or even laugh.

It wasn't until four years later that he found genuine reason to smile again.

He likened it to the first time they had made love, that time on Pentire Head at sunset, eleven years before. Except....

Raymond had removed his glasses, replaced his Faulks on the bedside table and turned off the light, all in one smooth reflex action. He lay for a moment as was usual reflecting on his loneliness and of the six happy years they had shared. Then, to the brief, rude sound of a motorbike roaring up his quiet Wimbledon street, he slid his body downward and pulled the duvet over his chest. He was almost immediately aware of something. Something strange. In the dark he could make out a hint of shimmering, like a distant horizon glimpsed through a heat haze. Just a hint. But it wasn't distant, it was right there in front of him, inches away. Raymond was curious but not the excitable type and stayed exactly in the position he was in to coolly regard the phenomenon. It took just a second or two to realize it was not just a trick of the moonlight, creeping in through some crack in the curtain. This was something altogether... odd.

He stared at the place where the shimmer seemed to struggle for existence, ethereal and fragile. His heart was pounding so loud he felt he might wake the neighbours. It was some time before he discerned a vague shape and then his heart almost stopped. It was surely a face; Trisha's.

Now it was his *head* that seemed to be thumping as the face, given sanction to exist by his recognition, gained in spectral form, then Raymond found himself lying directly under the ghostly, naked body of his beloved, though there was no sense of weight, sound or real substance.

"Trish?" he whispered.

There was no answer but now the being lying full length above him was unmistakable. He instinctively pulled the duvet away from him to allow their 'bodies' to meld together and lay there savouring the sweet melody of her presence. But there was nothing tactile in this apparition, he tried to hold her in his arms but although he could see her, there was no warm flesh to yield under his touch.

Her face was right next to his own, yet he could not find her eyes to drown in as he always used to. He tried to kiss her and found he had to hold his head back or he was stupidly pouting his lips somewhere in the back of her brain.

He did it: he held back and judged the position of his mouth to be over hers and felt the sweetness of her kiss as keenly as he ever did. They were drinking each other, yet there was no actual physicality.

He was amazed as he felt the familiar yearning of his body for her, the ache, the undeniable and irrepressible ache. His erection was full, urgent, and could not be denied and although they had not done this together for four years every movement was as instinctive and as natural as it had ever been. Together they gracefully twisted their bodies into position and, although he had to imagine her familiar purring and entreaties, for him it was just as if she was really there, in warm, full-bodied person. He was aware that nothing was actually touching, there was no physical sense of being inside her and no press of her soft, firm breasts against his chest: and yet there was. There actually was.

Suddenly he was spent, his body writhing in agony and ecstasy inside her and he felt his come spilling over his own belly and chest. He looked at the face beside him that he pretended to cup tenderly in his hands and he saw the faintest of smiles on the faintest of lips. He smiled back and then she disappeared. He felt strangely stupid, masturbatory, even used. But, as the thoughtful, philosophical man he was, he lay back pondering the experience as objectively as he could.

Yes, he had just fucked a ghost, a succubus. Or, at least, thought he had.

He considered and entirely discounted the possibility that it had all been his imagination. He was not an imaginative person, and anyway was enough in command of his senses to recognise the difference. He could because he was willing to. He could dispassionately discern the gulf between the real and the unreal. It mattered not to him which it was, because the only reality was the pleasure it brought him. With this slender evidence put to the jury, he concluded that the experience was genuine and he couldn't wait for the next one.

Unfortunately the encounter further wrecked his already tattered life. He had few friends, because he felt his company could never be described as entertaining. He had been permanently grieving since the accident and wanted to spare himself and others the charade of pretending to enjoy himself. One by one his friends had dropped away, unable to sustain a one-sided relationship. With all the goodwill in the world, one-sided conversations will eventually flicker and die like a Chinese lantern in a Force 9 gale.

His job had been his one salvation. He found it easy to discipline himself with all the demands an office job brings to bear. Getting up in the morning, because he had to, catching the Number 17 bus, because it was going where he had to go, sitting at his desk because his boss expected him to. Raymond carried out his duties at the insurance office efficiently and unhurriedly. It was the pattern of his existence that got him through, a somnambulistic drama and each day brought a curtain up, an interval and a finale. There were never any encores, no awkward requests to have a drink with a work colleague. Just home to his semi in the leafy suburbs, where he would prepare a small meal and then settle down to watch TV until bedtime at 10.30pm prompt. Then he'd read, fall asleep and stay asleep until 7.00am, when he would awake to re-enact the same lonely ritual all over again. It was easy. He didn't have to think. He didn't even have to want.

But now, for the first time in four years, he had something to actually *look forward* to.

And that made life even more awkward, his behaviour all the more erratic. At 5.00pm instead of shambling wordlessly and casually out of the Prudential building's swing doors he would hurry out blurting strange excuses to anybody who might be within earshot. He wanted to catch that first bus home. His office colleagues thought only a new lover could have brought about such a change in personality and they smiled knowingly at each other. But his work started to suffer too. Instead of ploughing through all his usual boring duties like a man asleep, he was indeed like the young buck yearning for moonrise. He couldn't concentrate and eventually his boss reluctantly considered the prospect of dismissal.

Raymond wasn't entirely sure that first time whether Trish would ever come again. Yet she did, a night or two later, and henceforth at odd, unpredictable times. He became adept at holding her shapeless, formless body in his arms as if she were flesh and bone. The sensation was all the same to him, such was his love and desire for her. He actually believed it couldn't have been any more 'real' if she was there in person. The kisses and the touching and the frictions were all in his imagination, he knew that. But it made little difference to him. To him she was really there in his arms.

She was always totally silent, of course. And no hint of the sexy aroma of her flawless white skin that he cherished so much when she was alive. All he had was the vision of her, and an extremely limited repertoire of facial expressions: a tender smile, lips half parted in desire. And something else. He sometimes detected a subtle, sad smile the melancholy of which tore out his heart.

But she kept coming, at all hours. Sometimes he would be sitting in front of the TV in the early evening and she would appear, naked as always, in his field of vision near the window. He knew then to turn off the set and she would come to him on the sofa. He marvelled that a man could achieve so much sexual satisfaction from the pure power of thought and visual stimulus.

Here, before him, was an image of the creature he loved the most and it was enough for him. Enough for his yearning body. He knew it was peculiar, but he never once craved for the actual touch of her hand, the physical pressure of her warm-blooded femininity. What he had he could hardly have dared prayed for. Enough was enough.

Once she appeared to him while he was making his Saturday lunch, or at least he thought she started to. As he busied himself at the kitchen table he spotted that now familiar shimmering in his peripheral vision. He stopped and turned to her. She seemed to stand there as usual in all her diaphanous beauty, and smiled serenely even as she faded. Perhaps she did not find his apron particularly erotic, he joked to himself. But, even so, he was bitterly disappointed that she had not stayed. It was the only time she ever did that and it left him nervy and bad tempered for the rest of the weekend. He wondered later if, on that occasion alone, he had simply imagined her.

Quite the nicest experience was when he had finally dropped off to sleep, convinced that she was not going to put in an appearance. Then he might awake in the early hours of the dark, deep morning with her lovely face before his. He had no concerns about his dragon breath as his heart lurched along with other parts of his anatomy. He loved those times best of all.

Eventually his long-suffering boss told him he had to let him go because his work had slipped into dangerous and irrevocable decline. Raymond found himself mooching around the house all day, disinclined to find other work and content just to await her pleasure. Every day, each and every entire day, was spent in waiting for her. He was happy. He needed nothing else.

But the day came, a year or so after his dismissal, when he did begin to long for something more from his succubus. The lack of physicality began to take its toll. He yearned to feel her fingers on him, he longed to taste her juices with his tongue. He needed to bite into those pure white shoulders her ghost only hinted at. He wondered, in his erotic passion, whether he needed the very control over her life and death that was denied to him now.

It was then he decided to join her in her deathly despair. Perhaps then they could whisper to each other in the night, as they used to. Perhaps the afterlife provided some of the accoutrements of the mortal world like warmth, words and wetness. He knew not, he could only hope. And so it was that one Saturday morning the milkman alerted his dairy who alerted the police that fifteen pints of milk were gathered like bottled snowdrops on Raymond's doorstep. By the time they found his body it was far too late to pump out several assorted varieties of sleeping pills and painkillers from his stomach.

Only three people turned up at his funeral service at a nearby Mitcham church: his former boss, the milkman, and the milkman's wife.

"Nice bloke," the milkman and the Prudential executive agreed. "Never the same since his wife died in that horrible accident. Scarred him for life."

But in our mortal ignorance, what know we of the comings and goings and social mores and customs of spirits? Does everyone become a ghost, or is it a state achieved by only a chosen few? Are we all reunited in death as some religious bigots assure us, or does loneliness exist on the other side as well as on earth?

Perhaps Raymond never found out. But in a small suburban bedroom in Wimbledon, a naked spectral figure was sometimes seen by later owners seated on the edge of the bed, her head bowed low and seemingly crying.

Others reported glimpsing her briefly as they busied themselves in the kitchen, preparing lunch at the table for their family. All these witnesses were touched by her solitary sense of melancholy, as if she was looking for someone, someone she couldn't find.

Black and White Rainbow

Black and white. This story is all black and white. Black and white because his whole world plunged into miserable black and white after Jessica's premature death in the Atacama. She loved the desert, as did he: a trillion shades of golden sunshine sand, melting into as many hues of orange and finally, a fierce, lusty red as the whole meets the impossibly blue ocean. What a mad, mad unlikely riot, when steaming dunes court cool, refreshing sea; yellow and azure, as striking as white filigree lace against deep mauve velvet, a piano keyboard, an atoll of purple jam on creamy semolina, even a grinning red Santa on a cake-top of white icing.

Jessica perished horribly amid those colours she so adored. Those colours died for James. He butchered them as they had butchered her.

Henceforth he spent his days in Lima in the depth of the dismal, foggy winter where he wouldn't be assaulted by the pale, pretty pastels of the fading colonial mansions, beautiful even in their dereliction. Lima tries to hide legions of them in surprisingly hushed and sombre squares with green parrots shaming the leaves on the trees; it is cheaper to let these old ladies die quietly than to restore them to their original glory. James never thrilled to them again anyway, loitering alone in the colourless slums, seeking a solace he could only find in the wispy embrace of the daily *neblina.*

Here he wouldn't be reminded of the rainbow palette that lured Jessica to a parched death in her merciless 4 x 4 furnace. She broke down in the middle of nowhere, no electrics, no water and the phone battery dead. She shouldn't have been there; she should have continued north on the Pan American Highway. She was on the last leg of her journey home, and presumably decided on impulse to have one more look at the desert when she reached Paracas. It was a fatal mistake. He could never forgive her for the utter stupidity of it, the careless contempt for precious life, losing hers and destroying his. Yet even in his anger he didn't see red, just a jet black void.

And now when summer comes and the colours demand to be noticed he flees to London or Berlin where the drab of winter still holds sway. Then as the inexorable grey threatens to lighten even these temperate cities, he seeks comfort in Helsinki, Reykjavik or Moscow. A sad, solitary figure, he mourns quietly and alone in Red Square on a dirty snow mantle sprinkled with hopping, black crows. Black and white. Black the colour of his heart and white the empty expanse that is now his life.

He watches a soldier in mud brown emerge smartly from his sentry box, turn sharply right, and goose-step heavily through the grey slush towards his comrade 50 yards away. Jessica also steps from the dark interior behind him, but unlike the soldier there is nothing military about her bearing. She glides towards James, slouching carelessly on the black iron railing. He doesn't change his stance, just stares dispassionately. She is dressed in the same travel outfit as when he had last seen her alive.

"Are you OK?" she asks quietly. He nods sullenly.

"You look..." she struggles for the word. He finishes the sentence for her.

"Lonely." This time *she* nods, then lowers her eyes.

"I think of you all the time," she says. "Up there."

"What's it like?"

"Up there? Gloriously light and shining white. This seems very dark and gloomy by comparison."

"Do you see colours? Do you see the colours of the desert?"

"Oh yes, of course. The whole spectrum, much brighter than here."

He remembers the glass phials he had been bought on the Isle of Wight as a child, filled with many layers of different coloured sands. He can feel a teardrop forming in the corner of his eye.

"Don't," she pleads. "I think of you all the time. Nothing changes. Love doesn't die..."

He wipes his eyes with his sleeve and when he looks again she is gone.

"It doesn't die here, either," he says out loud, and a mother standing nearby shoots him a strange glance and grabs the hand of her little boy.

"Only the colours. Only the colours die..."

James is a marine mining engineer, an oceanographer, and returns reluctantly to work with the hope of the hopeless, that he might continue his search for solitude at murky depths where the sun can't reach. Twelve months after his loss he is ordered to Mancora, hundreds of miles north of Lima on Peru's north west coast. There is a problem with an offshore derrick.

It is late afternoon and he sits on a dusty white beach, a straight whisky in his hand, staring at the black crabs scuttling among the rocks. He sees a bleak and black sky above, and a dark orb slipping sensuously and slowly into an ocean a drab shade of Guinness.

In his peripheral vision he is aware of her, there in the shadows at the edge of the trees, one leg bent with a naked foot resting coquettishly against the bark. He glances once but quickly turns away. She is wearing his favourite bikini. He can't see the colour but he recognises the pattern. In her hand she delicately clutches a dark cocktail which she is sipping through a straw.

"You have to let me go," she says quietly. "You know that."

He's going to listen to her, isn't he – to a woman who effectively killed herself through stupidity?

As he sits alone with his sombre thoughts, a child's cry pierces his resolute shell. It is a cry to wake the dead – and that is exactly what it does. He abandons the whisky to the sand and stands for a better view of the coast. At first he sees nothing but a distant white heron, disturbed by the sudden scream. He squints to focus on the gentle waves lining up in soft rows to sweep up onto the shore. And then he sees it – a wild splashing that can only mean someone in distress.

He pounds across the sand in his shorts, splashing through the shallow water at the ocean's edge, and then dives in expertly to meet the first of the breakers. The chilling scream continues in his ears even above the roar of the warm sea now obediently parting to accommodate his fast crawl. Within moments he has his arms around the limp body of a young girl, the breath stolen from her lungs by a violent threshing and thrashing under the waves. He senses the brute strength of a creature determined to drown its prey by dragging it underwater, just as a crocodile kills. He sees no croc, but something long and eel-like, the girth of his calf at its thickest. James lunges at it with one bare arm, the other around the girl to wrench her from its grip. Impervious to the bites and stings it inflicts on him he musters a desperate, super-human effort which eventually drives the creature off to the deeps to lick its wounds. James is left breathless and panting, doggy paddling in a sea tinged with three kinds of blood.

The child is barely conscious. With difficulty he swims with her back to the beach where a small crowd has gathered. He sweeps her up and wades to where a mother is pleading with outstretched arms and calling the child's name over and over again. Behind her, a father in a straw hat and a Hawaiian shirt timidly holds his wife's shoulders as James approaches.

"My God," says the woman, as she takes the child from him. "Haley…Haley…" she whimpers.

Someone has brought James an iced water as the huddle of people rushes Haley off with a waiting doctor. James takes it and falls to the sand, exhausted. It was the work of moments, but it drained him like the toils of Atlas.

Twenty minutes later a man appears back at his side. It is the girl's father.

"She's OK – thanks to you," he says, in a clipped New Jersey accent. "We were having a drink with friends over there at the beach bar. We didn't even know she'd gone."

James just stares at him, wondering what kind of parent doesn't know his child has slipped off for a swim as twilight approaches. She can't have been any more than nine.

"The doctor's treated her and she's asking to see you," the accent drawls, annoyingly. "You saved her life."

Without a word James allows the other's arm to coax him to his feet and lead him across the beach to the bamboo hotel. He is ushered into a small room where the doctor stands beside a bed. Haley is sitting up, all bright eyed, swathed in white bandages. She has been staring out of the window in wonder at the sun which is bidding its final farewell in golden splendour. She looks up eagerly as James enters.

"You saved girl's life," says the smiling doctor in broken English. "Just a few more seconds and…well, you know." He spots the deep gashes on James' arm. "I'd better look at that too, senor. You have both been lucky. Many dangers lurk in these seas…" He shrugs and trails off.

Haley is grinning cheerily up at James and gestures for him to sit beside her on the bed. Precocious American kid, he thinks, but does as she bids.

"Thank you, mister," she whispers. "I was so scared." He is surprised to find that she is hugging him, her good arm around his neck and her little head resting on his chest. They are both now gazing out of the window together like close friends, family even.

"Look at that beautiful sunset," she coos. "I might never have seen one again if you hadn't been there. Can you count all those beautiful colours – reds and orange and yellows? Every colour of the rainbow."

James finds himself smiling for the first time in an entire year. There is an unfamiliar, warm glow creeping slowly back into his soul.

"Yes," he replies. "I can. All the colours of the rainbow, tinged with gold… like a glorious Technicolor movie."

Sale or Return

Arthur knew he'd hit the jackpot. This was the fifth pub he'd tried and the first that hadn't immediately turfed him out on his ear. Elsie had lived around here before they married and told him more than once that in some of these ale-houses you could buy anything: unwanted kittens, sex, drugs, fake passports, clean driving licences – you name it.

The barman had given him a filthy scowl and put him firmly in his place. But unlike all the others, he hadn't told him to go away and do something physically impossible.

"Do I look like Doctor Friggin' Fix-it, some dog-turd dealer?" he'd barked pleasantly, turning his back to line up a newly cleaned tankard with others on the back counter. "Now can I pour you anything into a glass before someone breaks a bottle of it over your head?"

"Yes. Yes, please," mumbled Arthur. "I'll have a pint, please." He looked nervously around to scout for a suitable empty chair at a table. "Fuller's."

The stocky barman pulled the beer in silence and banged it down unceremoniously. He was short and tough with close-cropped hair which couldn't even try to hide an ugly, polished-skull piercing through his left lobe. His short sleeves allowed bulging, tattooed biceps total license to intimidate.

"Three pounds fifty."

Arthur took his drink to a hard chair at a table under a window. It was pitch black outside and the rest of Hackney kept itself to itself. Arthur could see only his own reflection and that of the sullen barman in darkened panes otherwise filled with notices for darts matches and live music nights.

Arthur was especially impressed by the invitation to TEST YOUR BRAINES AT THE D&D TOP QUIZ EVENING, FEBERARY 4TH.

What a battle of mental dexterity that promised to be, he mused. First Prize, one free lobotomy.

He kept his coat on but settled in for a long wait. He was a patient man. As a senior citizen, it was one of the few skills left at his command.

For almost an hour he sipped his beer at long intervals and guardedly watched the *Dog and Duck* clientele through hooded eyes, as surreptitious as a spy. It didn't pay for a stranger to invite too much eye contact in these places. Elsie had told him that. Snatches of conversation pierced his consciousness, jagged with ugly expletives. At last, he saw a man in a black, imitation-leather jacket go to the bar and speak to the barman who nodded in Arthur's direction. *Bullseye!*

"You mind?" The man was clutching a short, and yanking out the chair opposite Arthur as he observed what he evidently regarded as the niceties of East End etiquette. Arthur pulled a tight smile and made a small gesture with his hand to indicate his acquiescence.

The man sat there in silence for five minutes, apparently monitoring the progress of a pool game at the other end of the bar. He was youngish, about 35, tops, and suffered an unfortunate twitch that made his eyebrows flinch alternately as if he was permanently surprised, first by what he had seen out of one eye and then the other. Eventually, he turned his twitchy gaze to Arthur.

"I hear you may be lookin' for summat, summat special." His voice was edgy, nervous. Arthur judged that whatever it was he did, he wasn't terribly successful at it. The man dropped his eyes to his glass and swirled the amber nectar around before taking a deep swig. It looked like whisky.

"A gun," Arthur replied, in frank but hushed tones. "I want to buy a gun."

The whisky spluttered all over the younger man's face as he nearly choked. He wiped his mouth with a grubby red handkerchief.

"Keep it down, mate," he warned. "Walls 'ave ears."

"You asked," Arthur replied softly, his hands held together in his lap. Perfect composure.

"What exactly might you want this *item* for?" The eyebrows were going frantic.

"A crime, what else?" Arthur remained calm and matter-of-fact. "Do you really need to know the details? Do you care? Is morality involved here somewhere?"

Black jacket looked over his shoulder at the barman who was drying more glasses and theatrically avoiding his glance.

"Listen," he said, leaning conspiratorially over his shots glass. (If he'd had a tie, it would have been fishing for olives.) "I mean is it for a killin', or just for a hold-up… like a robbery?"

"I want bullets, if that's what you mean," replied Arthur, cool as a cucumber. "I don't want to wave it about and say 'bang'."

"Right joker, ain't yuh?" the other taunted.

"Not really."

Arthur remembered something unkind Elsie had once said to him in temper at their tiny, cramped council flat in Putney: *You used to be such a live wire, Art. Now you're just an embarrassing piece of faulty wiring in a big fuse box. You trip, we all trip.*

"You ain't plannin' to bump someone off, specifically? It ain't for a *murder* or nuttin'?"

He said the 'm' word like the dirty reality it was and Arthur was almost touched by his sensitivity.

"I need a gun and I need bullets. That's all you need to know."

"I might have what you need. But I can't dish these things out to just anyone. I need to know some *details*."

"How much?" Arthur was getting impatient.

"What sort do you want? A small *item*, or something with a bit more… clout?"

"A small one should do it. With shells."

"Could maybe get yuh a Beretta with a snub-nosed barrel. Very discreet. Fits in any pocket. Let's see now, with ammo – I s'pose we're talkin' 'bout a grand."

"Seven fifty!" Arthur began to sound to black jacket as if he were well used to this.

"I said a grand and I effin' well mean a grand," he replied. "You trying to take the pee?"

"It's all I've got. Seven fifty." Arthur patted his overcoat to indicate an inside pocket. It was an ASDA moment. "Got anything for that?"

Black jacket glared at him. "Depends what you plan to do wiv it. You'd better come clean otherwise no deal." He banged his palm on the table to emphasise his authority.

But secretly Arthur suspected it was just a sham. He paused and lowered his eyes before answering. After a few moments drawn out for effect he said quietly: "I want it for myself. Suicide."

"You only need one bullet for that," black jacket snapped back instantly. Arthur was impressed. Perhaps he was sharper than he thought.

"You have to allow for errors."

The other looked astounded. "You want to buy a gun so you can shoot yourself?"

"That's about it. Unless you want to do it for me. I could hire you to do the job, neat and clean."

Black jacket thought hard and long, rubbing his bristly chin thoughtfully.

"Ten grand. I'll do it for ten grand."

For the first time Arthur's elderly, wrinkled face broke out into a broad grin.

"I'm not going to pay you £10,000 for a job I can do myself for £750. I'm not even sure you could hit me the way you knock back that whisky." He laughed out loud.

"It's Jack Daniels."

This time it was Arthur's eyebrows that levitated in astonishment. "You expect a paying customer to buy you a drink?"

"I'd do a fine job. You wouldn't feel a thing. Ten grand and it's settled. You don't have to worry about getting yourself all couraged up. I'd creep in on you when you're least expecting it and… wham… you're history."

Grimly, Arthur chuckled again. "No thanks. I'll just take the gun."

There was another long silence.

"OK, give me 20 minutes. Opposite the pub is a side street, Carpenter Lane. First on your right down there is an alley leading to an old fountain. Used to be a horse trough or summat. Meet me there in 20 minutes." He got up to leave. "Twenty minutes," he repeated and strode across to the door.

Arthur sat where he was and finished the last dregs of his beer. He hadn't enjoyed any of it. Finally he plonked the empty glass on the table and struggled to his feet. His old limbs were stiff after such a long time in a wooden chair. As he walked towards the door he caught the barman looking at him. It was a cold stare, and Arthur could read nothing in it but idle curiosity.

He found the old stone trough easily enough, a rusty pipe still gushing a trickle of water noisily into what looked like a large, uncomfortable bath. It was a cold night but Arthur had a good feeling about this. It was all working out according to plan. He always was an optimist, unlike Elsie. She used to say the only good thing about being a pessimist is that you wake up each morning pleasantly surprised to find the world still here and in one piece.

She was sitting there now, right beside him. "You don't have to do this," she whispered. "Not for me." Her voice was crackly and broken. He ignored her. He at least wanted to get this one thing right.

Before long, black jacket was back, doing his best to conceal a brown paper bag crammed with contraband of a heavy nature.

They sat together on the rim of the trough, their illicit dealings poorly lit by an antique street lamp that looked almost as old as the stone edifice that was freezing their backsides.

A rustle of paper and the younger man pulled out a small, snub-nosed gun. Its black metal looked to Arthur like something very alive – sombre, and utterly serious.

"This is the Beretta," he said. "Short barrel, hides easy in a pocket or bag." He seemed to be considering something, his eyebrows bouncing up and down in the ghostly light like caterpillars in a sack race.

"Tell you what, on second thoughts," he went on as Arthur studied the gun without touching. "Why don't you just give me the 750 nicker now?"

Arthur could see that the grim object at first held up for his inspection was now pointed straight at his face.

"Hang on," he said as calmly as he could. "You're not going to shoot me for £750."

"How can you be so sure?" the other smirked.

"Because you said the going rate was ten grand, remember? Now you say you're going to do it for £750.That's a bit of a market free-fall, isn't it?"

Black jacket and his eyebrows looked confused.

"But you ain't *got* ten grand," he said finally. "I might be willing to take a pay cut, in the circumstances."

"I don't think you're prepared to commit *murder* –" Arthur stressed the word just as the other had earlier, "for a mere few hundred quid. Not with that barman telling the police he saw you and I sitting together all cosy and chatty. Besides, is it even loaded?"

Black jacket fumbled in the brown bag for the shells and held them triumphantly in his hand, bouncing them up and down gently on his palm.

"Wouldn't take a sec," he grinned. "But you're probably right. Ain't effin' worth it for a few measly quid. You're lucky I'm in a good mood. Just give us the seven fifty for the shooter."

"Well, actually," drawled Arthur slowly as he reached into the inside pocket of his overcoat, "this one *is* loaded. Recognise it?"

Black jacket's eyebrows were for once stock still as, united, they concentrated under a furrowed forehead on the long silver barrel of a revolver now in Arthur's hands and pointing menacingly at his heart.

"What… whaddya mean?" he stuttered. "Why should I recognise that thing?"

"Just a hunch," breathed Arthur slyly. "An old fashioned Colt 45, its serial number conveniently erased on a metal lathe. Six shots. Does the business, if a little messily."

Arthur was gratified to see that the younger man was visibly quaking. "I didn't know what she wanted it for, guv'nor," he pleaded. "I didn't know she wuz comin' after you wiv it."

"No, it was nothing like that." He smiled consolingly. "How much did she give you for it?" He noted that the other's cockiness had downgraded to extreme deferential. He was a shade disappointed.

"I dunno, guv. Maybe five, six hundred. I swear I didn't know she would use it on anyone. She just looked like some innocent old lady."

"Give her the first degree, did you? Like you did me?"

"Yeah, I asked her. I always does. She said she wanted it for protection or summat. That's it – she wanted it for protection. Otherwise I would never have sold it her, I swear."

"Small woman about my age, jet black hair? From a bottle of course." Arthur smiled reassuringly, although he was now holding black jacket's collar uncomfortably tight, and the muzzle of the gun was just inches from the other's nose.

"Yeah, that's her. Said her name was Lily and she was afraid of burglars. Said she lived alone in a rough neighbourhood."

"Her name was Elsie," whispered Arthur in his ear. "And the only roughs in her neighbourhood ran alongside the fairways at Hurlingham golf club. But she wouldn't tell scum like you the truth, now would she? She wanted it to blow her own brains out which she did pretty effectively late last night. She was worried, you see, about her failing health. She was depressed. Didn't want to be a burden."

"Honest, guv, I couldn't stop her. Now you say it, she did mention something of the kind, about being down. I'm sorry. I'm so sorry."

"Yes, I bet you are," Arthur went on quietly and smoothly. "But let's just treat this as a case of sale or return, shall we?"

Now the quivering wreck before him on the wall of the horse trough looked almost as puzzled as he was scared. "Sale or return?"

"Yes," said Arthur, cocking the Colt. "You made a sale and now I'm making a return. It's the bullets, see – she didn't need them all."

To the credit of the Hackney constabulary, the wail of the police sirens pierced the dark night less than fifteen seconds after a loud gunshot was first reported in the vicinity of Carpenter Lane and the *Dog and Duck* public house.

But before the officers of the Armed Response Unit could reach the body of a man in a black jacket, slumped lifeless and floating face up in a stone horse trough, local residents also reported the firing of a second shot, just a few moments later. Nobody noticed the small hazy form hiding in the shadows, a little old lady with jet-black hair softly tut-tutting under her breath. She had her arms outstretched as if welcoming someone, someone she despaired for, but loved nonetheless.

Footprints in the Sand

I am an impressive, regal, white bird, soaring with the thermals above a warm West African beach, the sky the myriad colours of sunrise. I am searching for something, someone. I am free, exultant in my freedom, but the pain of loneliness exterminates all else.

The rapping on the door was insistent and a rude reminder to get the bell fixed.

I rolled over and looked at my watch. 6.15am.

"Jesus."

The urgent banging of fist against glass went on. This wasn't the milkman.

"OK, OK, I'm coming."

I flung on my jeans and limped sleepily down the stairs to the door, rubbing my eyes with my knuckles.

"Jason Weaver?" The voice blustered from a ruddy-faced head atop a blue uniform. Other similarly attired intruders hovered rather menacingly either side.

"Yes. I think so, though I'm not sure. I was at my sleep."

"Can we step inside, son?"

She must have been four or five hundred yards away when I first saw her, and even across that vast expanse of early morning sandy beach I found myself physically attracted. It may be that the brain, given the merest hint of possibilities, conspires to assemble the available data to present what it feels is desirable. A sort of prescient wish fulfilment. She was little more than a dot nearly one third of a mile away, yet she was at that moment everything I could ever have dreamed of.

"What did you talk about? Do you remember what you talked about?" Trembling, pink, blotchy lips were mouthing a string of questions at me and I tried to fend them all off in turn as I busied myself pouring orange juice for four. They didn't want tea, these officers, they had spotted the freshly-squeezed juice when I opened the fridge. I'm a bit of a health freak.

"We didn't really say much. Just boy-girl talk. You know."

"No I don't. Tell me." He really didn't, I could tell.

“I asked her name. Marie. I told her mine. I asked her where she lived. She said she was staying with her uncle near the golf course. She asked if I played golf...”

“Do you? Play golf?”

“No. Well, I have... but no, not really. Cricket is more my game.”

“Cricket? Now that’s a strange pastime for a young Scot, do ye not think? Especially in St Andrews.”

I found an old pullover on the back of a kitchen chair and yanked it over my head, looking at him long and cool as soon as I was more properly dressed.

“I don’t think you’ll find anything especially Scottish about golf, either, officer – historically speaking. The Scots didn’t invent it. They adopted it. Traditionally, Scotland is more about clans than clubs.” I paused for effect. “Do ye not think?”

I was brought up mostly in Lochgilphead and came to this coast for the university but I was born south of the border in Chester-le-Street. I just didn’t want to tell him that right then.

For a moment there was an awkward silence before he cleared his throat and continued. “Her body was found on the fifteenth green. Do you know it?”

“No, I told you – I don’t play. Certainly not at St Andrews.”

“She’d been bludgeoned. Possibly with a club. Head all...” He decided not to go on. “Nasty business.”

He hid his distaste in his glass, which left shiny segments of orange on his upper lip. It was 7am and even wide awake I was suddenly giddy with garish visions of pink and orange and sticky red.

We turned to walk towards each other, each driven by some mysterious force which some romantics would perhaps ascribe to fate but the cynic in me would put down to good old fashioned sexual curiosity. Yes, hers too.

There was nobody else on that June beach, nobody for miles. Even the dog-walkers were still in bed. But she and I were drawn towards each other, two strangers beneath a dull Scottish sky flecked with lugubrious, tormented seagulls, two strangers deliberately changing direction across acres of sand so our paths would inevitably cross. What human miracle was this? What innocence, what careful order out of chaos? Two destinies closing like magnets because of the warmth of a mutual glimpse from 500 yards. Synchronicity, serendipity and sensual Odyssey.

"And that was the last you saw of her? On that beach, about..." he looked at his notes..."about 30 minutes after you met? You must have been the last one to see her alive – apart from the murderer."

"Yes, I'd say about 30 minutes, realistically. Romantically it felt like longer... the last thing I expected on a chilly Wednesday morning."

"Romantic?" I could see the word genuinely perturbed him. "And I think you mean Tuesday. The poor lass had long met her maker by Wednesday."

"Yes, yes of course." I was confused – all this was a bit much for my befuddled brain at that time of morning. "We had a rapport, a mutual attraction." I knew I was on dangerous ground here but I had no other path to follow but the truth.

"A *mutual* attraction?" The officer, the only one seated, looked at his companions, one male and one female. Both remained silent although the wpc shifted from one leg to the other. A sign of conspiratorial accord? I couldn't tell.

"How do you know it was *mutual*? Did Marie... *invite* you to follow her? Do you suppose she *wanted* you to follow her?"

I was fazed by all his emphases. It felt like a trap.

"I could tell we liked each other. But it was clear it was going to end right there, on the beach. We had explored our instincts, had a nice *chat.*" I tried a little emphasis of my own. "We touched base, so to speak. It was *exciting* and *nice* but that was all there was to it..."

"Exciting?" He was agitated by the word.

"Yes, exciting and *nice*." I hoped an emphatic stress in the right place would keep his dirty mind in order.

"Hello," she whispered when we finally met. It had probably taken about five minutes to reach each other. I responded with a similarly anti-climactical, "Hello."

Her eyes, soft and dewy with a hint of tear from the sand breeze, dropped coyly and gave me the chance to drink in her beauty. She was young, about 19, and long, mousy strands of hair fell to her shoulders in a careless, carefree style. Her white silken blouse billowed lightly above a pleated blue skirt, slightly too prissy for the beach. My heart raced.

"You're on the sands early," I said unnecessarily. "Easier to think without too many other people scuttling around, isn't it? Air's fresher too."

"I like people," she said, and the yearning in her voice instantly made me feel guilty.

"Oh, me too. But sometimes a clear beach makes for a clear head."

She smiled and I hoped I had redeemed myself. She drank me in whole with a gaze that melted me on the spot and in that moment proffered a candid vulnerability which insisted I take her in my arms right there and then. I resisted but felt my own insecurities meld with hers. I was probably just two or three years older but I knew instinctively she wanted me to 'protect' her. She needed to feel 'safe'.

"Imagine the loneliness of an empty beach for all eternity."

I was surprised and laughed lightly, slightly embarrassed.

"God forbid. But sometimes people can make the world feel a little cramped."

The pink-faced officer noisily plonked his glass down on the coffee table with a decisive bang.

"Do you know what I think, Jason?"

I hoped my silence and lowered eyes implied that I did not.

"I think... I think you tagged along with Marie, a little stroll across to the golf course... am I right?" I shook my head vigorously to deny the suggestion but I knew there was more – worse, much worse – to come.

"Then you got to the fifteenth green and you thought the mood was right for a little smooch, a little innocent kiss and cuddle let's say... nobody about that time of day."

"No!" I insisted. But he wouldn't stop.

"And then you realized you had misread her signals all along, she wasn't 'fair game' at all, as you young people say..."

Absurdly I wanted to scream at him that I didn't know anybody who would use the term 'fair game' in relation to romance, but instead I just kept shaking my head in panic. Fair game is a batsman's ball bowled too soft, too slow, not a girl found wandering alone.

"But what I don't understand is, where did the golf club come from? Isn't that what you used? Where is it now? Did you fling it in the pond – if so we'll find it pretty soon, you know? Forensics are standing by while they search the nearby greens, and that includes divers."

"Fair game?" I muttered weakly.

"Kiss me," she had said, and the shock lasted just a second or two. Guys like me are not programmed to miss too many golden opportunities like this. I held her in my arms for a while as our lips melted together but it wasn't long before we slipped to the pliant sand. We made love right there in full daylight, out in the open. I remember hoping that the dog walkers would stay in their beds a while longer.

Afterwards she gracefully rose to her feet and adjusted her clothing with admirable lack of fuss. As counterpoint, I dragged myself up with as much enthusiastic charm as I could muster, gushing pointlessly: "Can I see you again? When will I see you again?"

I drowned as those eyes held me once more in their enveloping, velvet grip.

"I thought you wanted to be alone? Just now you preferred an empty beach..."

"Empty – except for you," I stuttered awkwardly. "There has to be you."

"Well, there's not me," she said enigmatically. "There's just the empty beach." She vacantly surveyed the acres of yellow sand. Something strangely hollow in her voice and her expression perplexed me.

"Don't follow me," she said, and walked off back towards the town. "You may find me here again if you look. Or you may not."

The finality of her tone left nothing to be said and I watched in silence as she left me alone and afraid and feeling like a fool. For a while I made no move, my eyes burning into her back as she receded into the distance. I had hoped she would at least turn to wave but she didn't, and when she had disappeared, I sank to my haunches and turned my lonely gaze to the sea.

It was odd that she hadn't even waved, but there was something even odder too... something I didn't think of until later.

"Just the empty beach," I said quietly, and had to wipe a drop of moisture from my eye. The sand in the morning air had got to me as well.

"Is that how it was, Jason? Did you pummel her to death with a golf club because she wouldn't kiss you? Forensics will tell us all, you know. There's nowhere to hide. We know you met her because you told one of your pals at the pub. She made quite an impression, didn't she? More's the pity."

I got to my feet and stood there trembling. The wpc came to me and gently placed what seemed at the time a comforting arm on mine but I realized afterwards she probably thought she was restraining me. I was too perplexed to say or do anything. Nothing made any sense. I certainly didn't want to add to the mess by telling them *everything.*

They took me down to the station, of course, and I spent a night in the cells but they had to let me go pretty promptly the next day.

Police divers found the murder weapon, a buckled Number Nine iron, at the bottom of a golf course pond, but nothing linked it to any known member or player, and certainly not to me.

The talk was that Marie lived a very lonely life at her uncle's house and apparently often took long walks on her own across the greens. Looking for company, I can only suppose, remembering her last, sad sentiments about her yearning for people.

Forensic science failed to reveal any tell-tale sexual evidence. It was assumed she was battered to death by a maniac for no discernible reason.

There was some talk about charging me with wasting police time, impeding the course of justice, something like that. But it all came to nothing although they did send a priest to come and talk to me. He wanted to know 'every little detail' of my meeting with Marie. I wasn't sure whether it was for his benefit or mine. I'm not sure he believed me.

I can't truly get to grips with what happened, but I recognise the longing in my heart and I still fruitlessly scour those endless sands at daybreak hoping to see her face.

What I don't look for are footprints, for I finally realized what it was that was so odd when she didn't turn to wave goodbye on the beach.

I remembered my prints criss-crossed the sand in a crazy pattern but Marie hadn't left a single imprint anywhere, making me wonder if I'd imagined the whole episode.

Searching for a girl I know to be dead may be futile, but it is inspired by her own harrowing vision: the loneliness of an empty beach for all eternity.

Of course, they had to let me go. It turned out that I was right all along. Marie was murdered at around noon on Tuesday – while I was batting in the St Andrews First Eleven one-day match against a visiting English side. My memorable century was even recorded in the local paper.

Our romantic encounter was on the Wednesday – the day *after* she died.

The Luckiest Man in the World

The man was old, white haired and rheumy eyed, but there was an arrogant certitude in the way he took careful aim, eyeing up his target with a confidence normally only found in the young.

There would only be this one chance. It would have to be a lucky shot. But that was where his strength lay: he was The Luckiest Man in the World. He didn't need prayer and he didn't need skill. Skill and prayer were for the unlucky.

His every movement was watched by the hissing black viper, its swaying and lolling attuned to the movements of the man himself, or more particularly, to the small rock clenched in his right hand.

They were locked together in this dark, dank cavern, one of the deadliest reptiles known to the high Sierras and José, the Luckiest Man in the World.

A rock-fall had all but blocked the way out for the man, and the snake's one escape route was the hole it had slithered from; a hole it now most fervently wished to return to.

Hot sweat burned in the old man's eye but only the viper felt fear.

José Felipe Galera had always been lucky. It was the small things he noticed at first, like the day he ripped his brand new school cap only a week after starting his first class. He was five and he was fearful. The cost of his first uniform had been the chief topic of conversation for months. He had been left in no doubt even at that early age that his education cost his parents dear in personal sacrifice.

The small mountain village where he was born had two schools. Going to one meant you would stay a shepherd your whole life, and would learn to live with the heat and the dirt and the shit. Going to the other meant that you might one day climb down the mountain.

His mother had urged him to take great care with his crisp new uniform only that very morning. She had adjusted his bright red cap with such concentration that he knew with certainty that it was the crowning glory of his apparel. She kissed him as usual and he could see the pride glowing in her eyes.

Then there was the game, just like any other played at any school regardless of status or decorous uniform: a little rough and tumble natural to small boys, and the cap was ripped. The other boys stopped in their play and gaped. They too knew the cost their parents had to pay for education, and the value of its accoutrements.

José nursed the injured cap all the way home that afternoon, his little voice rehearsing his excuses under his breath. He was in for a backhander at least, perhaps even a strapping.

When he reached the bouganvillea within sight of his casa he saw his mother and father watching him from the terrace. His heart sank. They waved and he waved back, half-heartedly.

Between him and the house, the old shepherd was herding his flock of sheep along the road to his fields, and José noticed a buzzard hovering hopefully above.

He realized at once that the bird had its eye on a small, helpless lamb lagging behind its mother at the back. Worse, it was about to swoop.

He rammed his damaged cap on his head and ran yelling towards the lamb, sweeping it up it his arms just as the buzzard struck. Thanks to José, its fierce talons missed their mark but vented their anger instead on José's head before winging back up into the sky and safety.

He stood there dazed, with the tiny bleating lamb in his arms. His father and mother and the old shepherd came running anxiously to him.

"My chico, are you alright?" screamed his mother and inspected his scalp for injuries.

"You saved my lamb," announced the old shepherd gratefully.

"Well, that was some smart thinking," said his father. "How's his head?"

"Not a mark," replied his mother. "The cap's a bit ripped though."

"I'm sorry," whispered José.

His father waved a dismissive hand. "Of no consequence," he said. "Any hero will get his helmet scratched now and then."

The old shepherd was so grateful he kept the family supplied with shanks and cutlets for years to come and once his wife even wove a beautiful cardigan for José's mother.

José was not only saved a beating but hailed as a hero.

"Just lucky, I suppose," he thought that evening, as he settled down to sleep after prayers. He didn't think he needed to be grateful to any particular deity for this gift. It just was.

His luck held good throughout his school years. There was one occasion when he thought it had deserted him. On the day of his very important examinations at higher school, he was off sick with glandular fever.

There was no second chance, either you took the examination on the given date or you didn't. His parents were beside themselves with grief. His entire future had been wrecked by a fever.

But when from his sickbed he heard the shouts of glee from his classmates at the school gates he knew something had happened. The papers hadn't arrived at their remote mountain village and the exams had to be delayed for a week, by which time he was fit and well again. He passed with flying colours.

Just lucky.

When he was eighteen his thrifty parents spent all their savings to buy him a new car, so he could travel easily to his new job as a trainee estate agent in the nearest town some kilometres away.

"Please take great care of this automobile," his father had advised him sternly. "For it I have forsaken many happy hours with amigos at Diego's and it has also cost your mother several new dresses."

On the very first day he had driven the motorcar to the service station and asked the owner to fill her up while he went to the washroom.

Bruno, an affable, portly man, smiled and told him to leave it to him. He had that very morning taken on a new, young assistant Paco.

"Fill up the Fiat for José," Bruno had told him.

A few moments later Paco poked his head through the door and asked his boss a question.

"Do we do Red Cross diesel? He needs Red Cross diesel."

Bruno looked puzzled, peering over the top of his *El Monde* newspaper. "Never heard of it. Give him ordinary diesel. The pump on the end."

Some moments after that José appeared back in the cubicle and started fingering through his wallet.

"How much do I owe?" he asked Bruno, who put down his paper to consult his till.

"Ten pesetas. Diesel's a little more expensive, but it goes further," he beamed.

"Diesel?" José was distraught. He had heard how much it cost to repair petrol engines wrecked by filling up with diesel.

They both turned to Paco who appeared at that moment wiping his hands on a rag.

"My car takes petrol!" he screamed at Paco.

"But I checked on the fuel cap," whimpered Paco. "It clearly says DIESEL – with a red cross over it."

"That is a warning NOT to put in diesel, you donkey," yelled Bruno. "You're sacked. Go home."

All three rushed to José's new car parked outside at the pump.

"It's alright!" breathed Bruno. "The idiot has even got the nozzles crossed. He thought he was putting in diesel but you are safely filled up with unleaded."

"Does that mean I can keep my job?" Paco looked pathetically hopeful.

"Do you not know that two wrongs don't make a right?" Bruno asked him. "Be off home and don't come back. Vamoose."

Turning back to José he said, more kindly, "Please accept my apologies. You may consider this tankful as on the house."

Just lucky, I suppose, mused José.

His luck continued to hold out, after a fashion.

Two years later, as the region's newest and most successful estate agent, he wed the prettiest girl in the village. He alone survived the crash when the brakes on their honeymoon limousine failed in the mountains. The chauffeur and José's young bride were burned alive when the car plummeted over the edge of a cliff. José was miraculously thrown clear, unscathed, as the tumbling car erupted into a fireball – just lucky, everyone supposed.

Not long after that José drew the winning ticket in the national lottery and became a very rich man indeed. He set up a new home of his own in Granada in a select district near the AlHambra. He was lonely, but he was lucky.

On the day he left, his mother held his face in her hands and fussed over him just as she had on his first day at school. She fiddled with his hat as if it were still that proud, red cap. He could see the tears welling up in her eyes as she kissed him goodbye. His father too was choking with emotion.

As he drove away in his gleaming white Porsche, he knew he was leaving behind everything he had ever loved. He wondered how much he would miss them all – but consoled himself with the knowledge that he could always go back to visit. They would always be there, even if he was climbing down the mountain to go up in the world.

Exactly 48 hours later the entire village was devastated by an earthquake, the first in the region for 100 years. Every last soul of the population of 2,800 was lost in the quake and subsequent mudslide.

Just lucky, I suppose, screamed José inside his head when he returned some days later to the scene of the carnage. There was nothing to see. Just a new mountain of mud where his village had once stood.

Some years later José made new friends when he enlisted in the Spanish marines and his detachment found itself deployed in the Afghan desert with the UN.

It was good to have fresh attachments. It helped him forget. It helped him forget his astonishing good luck. But the memory came back to haunt him one searingly hot night in a frontline dug-out. He was there with Cpl Paolo, Juan and a few others. Brothers they were, in the heat of combat. Brothers until death, which came to visit them in the form of an enemy RPG.

Their command-post of comradeship became a screaming ditch of fire and scorched flesh. José watched the last of his friends die in his arms, his torn guts spilling all over José's lap.

Lucky José alone lived. He was sent home a hero, without a scratch.

His luck continued to curse him – even at the End of the World, when the hailstorm of H-bombs that everyone had feared for decades finally unleashed their terror. Armageddon had come calling but failed to find José.

Instinctively he knew he was the only human left alive when he crawled out of the secret catacombs deep beneath the ancient ruins of the AlHambra. He alone had sought shelter there when the final sirens wailed.

He had picked his way through the rubble that once was the grandeur of Granada and eventually found himself on relatively clear mountain roads, littered only with abandoned cars. None could be coaxed into life, their batteries and electrics rendered useless by nuclear fission.

In a ditch by the side of the road he found a horse, barely alive and incapable of standing. Its eyes were empty, scorched pit-holes. Three of its legs were separated from its body. He killed the piebald with a shotgun he had found in the ruins of a farmhouse. There was only one cartridge.

He eventually limped back to the region where his village had once stood, and found his luck waiting for him still. He remembered an artesian well so deep that its waters alone would be untainted by Strontium 90. He moved into a cave he remembered from his childhood. He was alive, the Luckiest Man in the World. The only man in the world.

This morning there had been the rockslide. He had woken to a low rumbling noise which was the mountain shedding its own tears of rock. He stared at the near solid boulder wall that had piled up at the cave entrance.

Had he slept outside as he normally did, he would have been squashed like a fly under a swat. But his fire had burned low around midnight and rather than taking the trouble to rebuild it he had retired instead to the warmer depths of the cave.

He smiled. A grim, severe smile. "Lucky," he said out loud.

Then he spotted the black viper and knew from childhood warnings that its fangs would kill as speedily as any poison.

At the same instant he spotted the hole the reptile had slithered from and to which it was now attempting to return.

"Mal suerte," he muttered, as he picked up a small rock in the palm of his hand. "Your home is here with me."

The rock sped from his fist and arced across the cave, its trajectory idly tracked by the hissing black viper, then lodged itself into the hole with a satisfying splat.

"Now it is time for you to change my luck," he said as he rolled up his sleeves.

José offered up his bared arms as he approached the suspicious, slippery fiend.

"Aqui, por favor," he whispered and grinned a satisfied grin. After all, wasn't he the Luckiest Man in the World?

Top Table

He ceased to struggle the instant he sobered to the realization that if the immense winged creature above actually let go he would plummet thousands of feet to certain doom among the grim, forbidding mountain peaks below.

It was black and vulture-like, this creature, like a condor, but more than twice the size of any he had ever seen in the Andes. Its talons were as big and powerful as dockyard crane hooks and his near naked body hung like a rag doll crumpled and awkward in their clutch. His desperate efforts to escape had left his entire length flayed and striped with blood-red weals, but his groin and his waist where the giant talons gripped were worse. His back, too, felt as if it were about to snap. The bitter, high-altitude winds thundered in his ears yet, absurdly, his iPod still clung to his neck and dangled precariously below him, one earpiece close enough to emit the tinny thrust of Tchaikovsky's Cossack Dance.

"Don't be so damned arrogant, John!" Georgina was losing it big time, but then she always let people get under her skin, especially John. To his credit, his feathers remained unruffled. Only Matt and Josie broadcast alarm bells to each other with one fleeting but knowing glance. Matt grimaced into his glass of Sauvignon.

With an exasperated grunt somewhere between a spit and suicide, Georgina smacked her own forehead with the palm of her hand.

"God, you really are the most smug, complacent bastard I have ever met."

John raised his glass to toast his own wickedness. "Blame yourself, darling," he grinned devilishly. "You have given me every single thing I ever wanted – where else was there for me to go but the land of smug complacency?"

The giant bird swept down onto a small rocky plateau just a few feet across, and dumped John's broken body on the edge of a drop deep enough to stack dozens of Empire States. The bird stood beside him, towering at more than man height as it preened its wings. He lay motionless on the ground watching it carefully. The monster bird knew its prey was secure, there was no chance of escape; except down to certain death.

John inspected the giant talons, stained with his own blood, and was struck with a chilling realization. The bird could have killed him at any time – one tiny squeeze and he would have been history, Man-Jam. The behemoth was keeping him alive on purpose; it wanted its meat fresh. John peered over the lip of the precipice and felt dizzy with vertigo. He struggled to his feet and instantly whipped his hands to his face as the bird lunged its foot-long beak at his eyes.

"Jesus, you're trying to blind me," he shouted out loud, but he was also aware it was deliberately keeping its strength in check for fear of tipping its dinner into oblivion.

Nonetheless, time and time again the beak lunged at him until his hands were stripped of flesh. He dropped to his knees to hide his eyes from the creature and only then did the assault stop. John peered through his bloodied fingers at the sight before him; a *brilliant blue sky with other winged creatures soaring nearby, some perhaps as large as this one, the reason he was so jealously guarded by his captor. There was only one emotion stronger than the pain that wracked his entire body from head to toe; fear. Fear of what was going to happen next. The two watched each other suspiciously, yet John could detect a confidence in the other's eyes, a cocky confidence he himself could not possibly muster.*

Matt coughed gently. "I think, to be fair Georgina, all John was saying was that as we are pretty much at the top of the food chain, we should at least be grateful and enjoy it."

"I think, to be fair Matthew," mocked Georgie in a comical falsetto. "All John was saying was that vegetarians are lily-livered liberals who deserve to be gobbled up by the first thing on four legs to call them Dinner."

John laughed and with some relief Matt and Josie downgraded the alert to Amber.

“I’ve heard Victorian women actually hoped they would find themselves pretty hosts to a tapeworm, to keep them eternally slim,” he rejoined.

“Oh my God,” exclaimed Josie, her face suddenly shock-white and clasping her open, slack mouth with her hands. “How would you ever be rid of it?”

Matt joined in the fun. “Don’t be daft, woman – when it had done its job it slithered off down to the nearest Burger King for a decent meal.”

“You veggies are just like that,” persisted John, his cruel streak running away with him. “Your sweet-n’-lows and rabbit food low-calorie lettuce lunches are your modern-day tapeworms.”

“Ugh!” Josie exclaimed, disgusted, pushing the last of the celery to the centre of the table.

“It is the natural order of things for man to eat meat. We are all predators and there is no place for guilt-ridden weeping and wailing.” John paused. “Besides, I like my tenderloin.”

“You might feel differently if you were swimming around at the bottom of the pond,” Josie chimed in, more to offer Georgie some feminine back-up than to rekindle the argument.

“A sprat instead of a prat,” whispered Georgie in a snide sotto voce.

“Nonsense,” replied John, leading with his chin. “I simply respect the intended order of things. As a sprat I would go willingly to the shark’s table.”

Georgie knew instantly she had him. Victory shone vicious in her eyes like neon napalm.

“Ah… so you’re telling us that if a big hungry lion stumbled upon you without your equalising fire-stick you would lie down with your paws in the air and say ‘Bon appetite, Leo, I think I would recommend me medium to well done, but I guess you’ll be having me rare.’ I don’t think so.” Georgie looked at Josie with a satisfying ‘get-out-of-that’ gleam. Even Matt raised an appreciative eyebrow as the sisters high-fived.

But John wasn’t beaten yet. “Leo may be big but he’s wrong if he thinks he’s higher up the food chain than me,” he responded. “I’d simply enlighten him to the fact that the female of the species is far, far tastier and suggest a suitable sauce to supplement your beautiful hide.”

Luckily there was nothing heavier than an unwanted bread roll left on the table for Georgina to throw at him and it bounced off harmlessly as Matt and John slapped their own gleeful high-five.

The next day Matt drove the girls into the nearest town for the market while John poured himself into his £100 Calvin Klein swimming shorts for a serious tan session by the pool. It was hot and it was peaceful and he had enjoyed his huge sausage and bacon breakfast which loomed menacingly over Georgina's yoghurt and banana. Even Matt baulked at the Black Pudding.

"Put hairs on your chest," John had taunted him. "If they could find a landing strip wide enough to take root, that is."

For the umpteenth time he turned over onto his stomach, his iPod earphones exploding with the 1812 and his imagination grappling with the latest Murakami. He could feel the soothing caress of sunshine on his back and his calves, as intimate as any lover's touch. It was February and the Bolivian high summer sun still burned fiercely in the sky, trying to melt him into his plastic sunbed. Their borrowed villa was high in the mountains, a long way from the claustrophobic chaos of La Paz. He was totally alone with the cicadas and the humming birds and his rum punch, mixed just the way he liked it.

He shivered, a little bad tempered, as something big momentarily blocked out the sun, creating a deep chill that sank deep into his soul.

He screamed in pain beyond any he had ever suffered as the creature sunk its talons into his midriff and took to the skies again. The bird answered his cry with a decibel-busting cry of its own – an unholy squawk not of terror, but of triumph. John's eardrums all but burst and he tore the remains of the iPod leads from his head and threw them back into the empty skies below. As he did so, he noticed the bones in his fingers were showing through the bloody mess that was the torn flesh of his hands. He felt sick. Somehow he managed to turn his head and retched into the void beneath. Then, mercifully, he blacked out.

He awoke to find himself dumped unceremoniously on another cramped plateau, this one supporting a prickly nest containing three of the creature's young. The chicks were themselves almost man height and squawked and screeched with delight over their drop-in dinner.

Interwoven branches scratched and scraped his already battered body as he tried to hunker away to the very edge. But there was only one escape – and first he had to scale the thick trunks under the watchful eyes of the creature and its hungry brood. Several times he screamed in pain as beaks pecked deep into his back but desperately he kept going. How he wished he had simply jumped off into the abyss at their first resting place. Nothing could be worse than this.

Miraculously he withstood the merciless barrage and made it to the top, to fall gratefully off the side into the blue unknown. He even managed a grim smile as his momentum gathered speed and he felt himself falling... falling... falling...

"Do you think we'll always be at the top of the food chain, I mean with evolution and all that?" Josie had asked innocently that previous evening.

John snorted and waved a dismissive hand to the heavens, where the night was already deep and black. "The moon's drifting out of earth's orbit at something like half an inch every year. That big sun up there is sitting around waiting for a good day to explode. Whenever either of them goes, we go. Nothing lasts forever."

"Except your bloody penchant for pomposity," sneered Georgie under her breath.

As he plunged into unstoppable freefall, the grotesque squawking faded into the distance above him. But even as he tore through the endless nothingness, he was convinced that at any moment he would awake to find himself in his soft bed with Georgie by his side. 'Too much red meat and too much red wine for dinner, that's all,' he thought.

He always was a smug, complacent bastard.

Buy Me, Get One Free

Moon-eyed street waif fumbles with deceased mobile phone buttons battery ran out in June credit months before nobody ever calls anyway here in Lidl's trolley park her current no fixed abode rolling a funny one on her own in the dark mumbling something can't quite make it out over the splattering rain on the pinkish plastic roof what's that she's saying? *Buy Me, Get One Free.*

Shadow man oh mad man bad man downers weighing heavier than uppers hands in pockets one counting amphetamines the other scratching balls hissing steel pissing fire wants waif no love just wants wants wants. *Hey Up!*

Helter Skelter, we know you're gonna belt 'er Connie Ronnie Johnny and Bonnie see all feel nothing aggresh on street not Kool breathe Kalm Kalm take a toke and leave her be Monster Man Connie coughs.

Moon-eyes tries to look like Monroe big eyes struggling to sparkle wanna share my shelter and my toke Big Shadow Man one damp quarter inch left wanna drag 'scuse lipstick but there ain't none laughs laughs laughs shivers in Shadow of Shadow Man.

You want pills green yellow blue I got pills let me pull up a trolley got no place to go but here sing me a song Moon-eyes you can lean on me and suck my pills green ones yellow ones blue ones 'til you sleep.

Connie Ronnie Johnny and Bonnie see all feel nothing 'cept the rain on their pain leave her 'lone Rat Man we're comin' to get you.

Moon-eyes laughs trembling fingers place her toke between his lips suck on this stranger 'til I fall in love please be with me this rainy night he laughs he laughs he laughs *WAIT*.

His Shadow reaches into her deep deep deep she shudders stops laughing and cries inside where she's warm and it's Sunday with Mum's roast crackling in the oven. Help Me don't take my warm I'll pray to your god but his Shadow is all hands black and grabbing Let Me In It's Home In Here.

Connie Ronnie Johnny and Bonnie take a splash step through the puddles hoodies hiding their faces from the rain and the night Back Off Shadow Man.

Moon-eyes sobs into his devil denim I 'ain't had a shoulder to lean on forever but yours is ice cold Are You The Deceiver? Shhhh, Shhhh, Shhhh... his blackened hand strokes the back of her hair bleached blouse torn jeans Christ a crucifix Shhhh I am The One the one you get the one you got.

She shakes she surrenders she knows the Day Is Come deep inside her Sunday has fled it is Monday Black Black Monday full of Double Maths broken launderettes JobCentre Inquisitions lost hope faded memories second hand Tampax only-one-careful-owner used condoms and the Shadow Man I Am Ready.

Satanic sneer over black teeth which bite but never taste Sing Me a Song Moon-eyes I can't negotiate until you open a door part your lips and let me hear your invitation Feel My Breath fresh as Spring only not this last one.

Connie Ronnie Johnny and Bonnie see all feel nothing 'cept the rain on their pain leave her 'lone Rat Man we're comin' to get you.

The Shadow sees four shapes in the corner of his eye floating across a dark car park where four by fours and mothers will shortly reign when day begins but now it is His Land and a prize is in his arms waiting for his knife like she waited last time in the park when it was Christmas and the trees hung heavy with sorrow and dirty snow It Is Now.

Pop Music Pop Music Everybody's Talkin' 'Bout Pop Music her voice is faint but he can hear her over the rain she is letting him in I'm comin' I'm comin' I'm comin' please don't close the door never mind these floating shapes they just want to spoil the fun This is Our Kingdom and It Is Come what do you think of my steel blade it is as cold as your heart.

New York, London, Paris, Munich… my heart ain't so cold as your hands and your breath I want to go back home to Sunday and Mum's roast please don't make me stay on this Black Monday where the world is curling up to die it is so dead I can smell the formaldehyde on your tongue spare me spare me Shadow Man.

He hisses at the four shapes lurking just by the trolley park this is not your place go go go to where the rain will wash you away I am King and you are scum I stand here dry with the world in my arms while you only lurk and gape Behold Me.

Moon-eyes struggles but she cannot escape the iron clutches which envelope her every organ and limb I didn't mean to sing it was a mistake let me go and I will hum you a love song my daddy used to cry over please please please take these chains from my heart.

Connie Ronnie Johnny and Bonnie see all feel nothing ’cept the hate in the Shadows and the Fear in the Shade we will not walk away Shadow Man we are the Executioner’s Executioner we will not let you weave your evil where evil has already woven Listen To Us Listen To Us.

Shadow’s blade swipes and glistens in the faint light still damp from a dozen sacrifices This Is A Warning see my razor edge and my sharp point to make you all bow and listen Beware.

Moon-eyes breaks free but sees only Death glinting in the rainy moonlight You Could Have Shared the Comfort of My Sunday fire why steal my empty life for your empty dreams when I give you the last quarter inch of my reefer.

Connie Ronnie Johnny and Bonnie see all feel nothing but the catch of breeze as the blade brandishes death before them a sharp intake of breath and their faces stop time frozen as Moon-eyes stares at the knife and Shadow Man glowers at the four shapes.

He can’t see their faces under their hoodies he can’t see their lips move but he hears on the wind *We’ll Huff and We’ll Puff and We’ll Blow Your House Down.*

As one their breath dispels in a gust and Shadow Man vanishes to dust, his presence vaporized. The blade clatters on the flagstones erect but impotent. She stares into darkened cowls can’t see their eyes. *He was my man you ferkin’ freaks*, she screams. *He was just looking for shelter where he could hum old Oasis hits. There’s a brat in my belly I forget who put it there but nobody will keep us out of the gutter now.*

They turn and walk away through the murk and the rain it is the darkest hour before dawn but soon this bleak car park will fuss with mothers and prams and reversing Renaults and hollow-faced shoppers wielding their trolleys just like the cow catchers on their giant black-windowed Cherokees. *I’m coming through schmuck get out of my way ‘cos this cold steel battering ram is coming through first.*

Moon-eyes will be gone with the first shaft of gloomy light but the rain will still be here.

Angel

For the hundredth time, Harvey checked the placings. The serviettes were folded exactly the way she liked them and the cutlery set just so. He slid her wine glass two inches to the right and then back again. He brushed imaginary crumbs from the seat of her hardback chair. He was humming one of their favourite tunes. A song about love and loss and how they went hand in hand somehow. He felt sure the moon came into it too but he couldn't exactly remember the line.

Moon. June. Out of tune. He smiled.

His heart, he realized, was fluttering like a schoolboy's on a first date. On his way back to the kitchen he once again appraised his appearance in the mirror. Older, certainly, but there was a certain savoir faire. A mature sophistication. No dandy, but no fop either.

On the kitchen stove the *coq au vin* was coming along nicely. He added a little salt, just a dash, and breathed in the fumes over the saucepan with a satisfied air. "Perfecto," he said out loud. "Exquisite."

He knew the whole charade was just that, a highly elaborate primal mating ritual with only one design in mind: to win the girl. Angel played along. She truly appreciated his efforts, just as nature intended. She would smile demurely, allowing him to pull out the seat for her at table, fussing and cooing like an old mother hen. No, not like a hen. Just the opposite – a strutting cock, a rampant rooster. He laughed at himself and knew his thoughts would amuse Angel too. They had no secrets, these two. They were as close as any lovers could be. It was OK with her if he wanted to play out his little tableaux of courtship. He could show off his fanned feathers and dance on the bough as much as he wanted, it was all the same to her.

She was just happy to fall into his nest, was Angel. Let him play his games.

There was a knock at the door, a soft rap, *her* knock. Harvey looked around in a panic, wondering where to throw the Sydney Opera House tea-towel draped unromantically over his arm. Couldn't answer the door with that. He stood at the entrance of the kitchen and threw it haphazardly towards the work surface.

She stood there like the dream she was. Her soft, chestnut hair dropping gracefully over her shoulders allowing just the tiniest sensual hint of neckline. He loved every part of her. Even her earlobes. *Especially* her earlobes he mused now, as he admired the way the flesh of them peeked out between the shining, multihued strands of her hair.

"You're here," he breathed unnecessarily.

"Well, that's a relief. I wouldn't mind betting that's why you opened the door." She walked past him into the house and immediately took in the elaborately laid out dinner table. *He* took in the heady, captivating scent of her perfume: his favourite. *Je Revien* by Worth.

"Expecting someone?" She teased him mercilessly, her gentle, warm smile at once lending the lie to her playful sarcasm.

"Nobody I wouldn't die for. Champagne?"

She nodded and threw back her head with that almost childish abandon that sent shivers through him. Her hair, a thousand shades of brown and red, shimmered in the artificial light as it sought to settle once more on her shoulders. She was wearing her red dress. *That* red dress.

He knew she wouldn't be wearing anything beneath it.

"Champagne?" she urged coquettishly, as he stood transfixed for moments longer than was polite.

"Of course." He hurried to the table and took the bottle from the ice bucket, trying to keep his hands as steady as he could as he poured two glasses.

"Easy," she coaxed, still playful. "That stuff will play havoc with your doilies."

They smiled, lovers' smiles, and linked arms to toast their intimacy.

"I love you," he murmured, more concerned with her glistening, moist lips than the rim of his champagne flute.

"Only half as much as I you, you dog," she giggled, and thirstily struggled to bring her glass within range of her mouth. She drank and he watched transfixed as her throat rippled voluptuously around the liquid slipping down deep, deep inside her.

He didn't want champagne. He wanted her. But the game had to be played. There were rules, even between the closest of couples. *Coq au vin* would win this round.

"Smells good." Angel laughed as she broke away and seated herself at the table. "Let's eat and then we can think of something else to do." She shot him a warm, sensuous smile that fired him to the bone. He wished he had phoned for a pizza.

"*Coq au vin*," he announced cheerily, putting down his champagne. "Coming right up."

He stepped briskly into the kitchen and tended to the oven. Angel had risen from her chair and now came right up behind him, encircling his waist with her fragrant, feminine arms. Like that schoolboy, he could have fainted with overwhelming love and desire right there and then.

"What's your Sydney Opera House tea-towel doing wrapped around your toaster?" she giggled in his ear.

"Keeping the toast warm, of course. Get back to the table while I serve up."

Obediently she released him and at once he felt the frosty chill of reality, despite the radiating burst of heat from the oven.

As Angel returned to the other room sweetly singing soft love songs to herself, Harvey took the tea-towel to protect his hands opening the oven door.

"Roast potatoes ready to go. We have lift-off," he called back to her.

Suddenly there was a rapping at the door.

"Jesus. Who can that be?" he muttered bitterly, closing the oven door, bad temperedly switching off the heat from both the oven and from under the saucepan. He marched smartly back out to the other room.

"Probably Sammy. You'd better hide in the bedroom while I get rid of him," he barked impatiently. Angel obeyed immediately without question.

Sure enough Sammy stood there at the door, alone but laden with a heavy looking cardboard box.

"Hi Dad. Cindy thought you might be in need of provisions."

He stepped in and walked over to the table where he put down the box and began to remove some items for inspection.

"Canned peaches – your favourite. Ambrosia creamed rice. Frozen broccoli. Some of this stuff will have to go straight in the freezer."

Sammy studied each offering as if seeing it for the first time, before placing it all on the table.

"Oh, expecting a guest?" he asked, seeing the extravagantly laid table before him. "Is that pizza I can smell?"

His father said nothing, hoping his stony silence would ensure that this was a quick visit but Sammy was in no hurry and began to take some of the foodstuffs through to the freezer.

"Ah yes, definitely pizza," he called, as he loaded up the empty shelves. "Hawaiian special with anchovies and pineapple, if my nose does not lie. You don't look after yourself, Dad. There's hardly anything in here."

"I get by." His father's tone was sullen, unwelcoming.

Sammy re-emerged from the kitchen and took his father by the shoulders so that he could steer him to sit on the sofa. He perched himself beside him.

"What are we going to do with you, eh? You don't call, you don't visit. Cindy's worried you don't eat properly."

"So I see. I don't need all that stuff – I can get what I want from the supermarket. I'm not a cripple."

"You don't shop for anything but takeaway pizzas, Dad. Anything you can order up on the phone. Come on, you can't go on like this."

Harvey pulled an exasperated face, linking his fingers before him on his lap, which Sammy recognised as his hermit's leave-me-alone signal. It could have been in letters ten feet high and neon lit.

"I'm fine."

"Dad. It's been ten years now. Life's got to go on. Mum wouldn't want you skulking away in a corner for the rest of your years. We all love you – but it's so hard to get you to spend time with us."

"Don't tell me what Mum would have wanted. She didn't know herself what she wanted. Otherwise she wouldn't have..."

"Dad, Dad, Dad." Sammy could see that his father was getting upset and put his arms around him and drew him near. "Don't dwell on it, pops. She was confused. You know what the doctors said...."

"The doctors said she died from asphyxiation. If the rope hadn't killed her, the pills would have."

"I didn't mean that. I mean about her state of mind. It wasn't so much that she was *unhappy*, her brain was becoming bewildered. She was in a very dark place and couldn't cope. She wasn't unhappy with *you*. Or us for that matter."

At that Harvey broke down and buried his face, sobbing, against his son's shoulder.

"Angel!" he wept. "My Angel!"

"Shhh, Dad. Shhh. Everything's OK. She's happier now. And I know she still loves you, all of us. But you have got to get on with your life. She would want that."

"If she wanted that she wouldn't have hanged herself, would she?" Harvey's tone changed abruptly. He became sharp, abrasive, accusing.

"She didn't know what she was doing, Dad. She didn't want to hurt us. Her poor muddled brain was in a turmoil. But she's gone and we're still here."

"Leave me alone, Sammy." It was all he said, but somehow Sammy knew he meant it. He stood up to leave and looked at his father one last time, a long lingering gaze.

"Not going to share your Hawaiian special with me, then?"

"Leave me be, son. I just want to be on my own. I'll be OK. I'll call you soon. Maybe at the weekend. Thank Cindy for the supplies."

Sammy judged his mood to be a little brighter and, after hesitating a second or so more, gave him one more hug before he said his goodbyes and left.

Harvey sat there on the sofa with his head buried in his hands. But suddenly he lifted his face, his nose urgently sniffing the air.

"God, the *coq au vin*!" he exclaimed, and hurried to his feet calling loudly: "You can come out now, Angel – he's gone."

She stood at the open bedroom door, her right hand resting vampishly against the frame high up near the lintel, her left akimbo against her hip. She was totally naked and inviting, her beauty unblemished, except for the weeping, red weal completely encircling her throat.

Each Breaking Dawn

St JUST, CORNWALL. Friday June 16th, 1999, five days after leaving Eriskay in the Scottish Western Isles

It was the toughest moment of her life. After all the Jezebel lapses born of pure selfishness, this was Gemma Fairweather's come-uppance. She was trembling so badly she couldn't light her cigarette and gave up the attempt.

Incongruously, mid-summer bees droned pleasantly. Birds were singing, and she could hear the occasional traffic politely whispering past just yards from the garden gate she had been careful to close, cutting off her own escape. All else was silence, a deep, grave silence to remind her she stood there accused. She shook her head to clear the doubts before ringing the doorbell.

Twenty years of guilt hung heavy on her mind as, tall and elegantly dressed, she waited by the cottage door. The combined scent of hibiscus and jasmine was heady enough to make her faint but it was the fear that made her giddy. What would she say? How can you express two decades of contrition?

"Annabelle, treasure, I'm so sorry – I should have written, phoned at least."

It all sounded so trite.

The door opened and a little girl in a buttercup yellow frock stood before her, gazing abstractedly. Gemma was shocked, this couldn't be right.

"Annabelle?" Then she blushed at her stupidity. Of course, this would be Annabelle's own daughter. A happy looking girl of about eight, a wealth of curly scarlet hair falling to her shoulders, cradling a black and white kitten in her arms. She was about the age Annabelle had been when Gemma walked out.

"You want Mummy," she said, and darted back inside the cool, rather gloomy interior. Gemma tried to peer beyond but could perceive little but a sense of cluttered furniture, perhaps a Welsh dresser straining under Capo del Monte and faded, willow-pattern dinner plates.

A figure appeared just where the little girl had vanished in the dark recesses of the hallway, a young, beautiful woman in her late twenties. She was wiping her hands on an apron and staring quizzically at Gemma. After a moment her expression lurched from slight bewilderment to utter disbelief.

"Mum?" It was the red hair, common to them all.

Despite the years, despite the unknowing, despite the hurt they had both keenly felt, they fell into each other's arms.

"Annabelle," Gemma wept. "Not a week goes by..."

She explained as best she could, about the irresistible temptation of a new, exciting romance after years of loveless tedium, how she'd always meant to write, how her heart was broken, how she suffered constantly from what she had done.

Annabelle seemed to take it all philosophically. There were tears but there were no recriminations. Old photographs were dug out of drawers and pored over amidst the tea and cake crumbs, happier memories now mostly kept hidden alongside forgotten Christmas candles and pointless, redundant keys. And afterwards everyone, including the little girl, whose name was Mabel, seemed the better for it and with a new, lighter heart Gemma could finally face the future.

They were full of promises, promises neither of them could have kept, drunk with rash assertions that nothing mattered, only that they had found each other again. There would be visits, shopping expeditions, new unforgettable reunion dates scrawled in deep red on calendars.

Mobile phones were tapped wildly as numbers were exchanged and entered into hallowed lists of personal contacts, text messages would henceforth scurry back and forth with abandon. They were mother and daughter again. Mabel even slipped a little gift into Gemma's hand as she left: a Swiss mountain maid finger-puppet with impossibly rosy red cheeks and a bright blue bonnet. Then she sweetly recited a poem her mother had taught her: *Each breaking dawn is but yesterday's tomorrow and tomorrow's yesterday.*

After all the misery of twenty dark years, the Fairweather family would once again sail calm and happy seas.

Gemma's heart was brimming with happiness as she drove away smiling and waving with ridiculous ardour. Annabelle returned her farewells with a heartfelt gusto that would allow none of the bitterness and anger to emerge.

The barefoot path to repentance had been trod, a route Gemma to her eternal shame had been quite unable to negotiate for two decades, and she was overjoyed to pull away with nothing but warm, loving smiles in her rear-view mirror. Her immense sigh of relief as she sought out the first Cornish signpost that would lead her back home might have deafened the gods. It was a Friday to remember, on the eve of the New Millennium, and from now on not a week would go by without it being celebrated.

After a few hours she cursed herself for not asking if she could stay the night, but there had been a special magic that somehow she didn't want to sully with such practicalities. She began looking for a B&B along the ever-darkening roads as she crossed the Devonshire border. Fields of bright golden corn turned mustard and dull in the failing light but as she swept past the occasional tractor she could still admire the picture-postcard villages, alive with tea shops and quaint cottages, the antithesis of the bleaker Cornish terrain she had left behind.

Cautiously she overtook a dirty yellow cart pulled by a large shire horse, a curiously old fashioned young boy leaning on a shovel in the back, his young sister in a drab, grey skirt on her haunches beside him. Both children stared defiantly at her, the boy derisively wiping his nose on a grubby sleeve.

Gemma, unnerved, struggled to concentrate on the road and within seconds was astounded to have to pull out around an exact replica of the cart, also pulled by a plodding shire.

Already stunned by the coincidence, she found herself followed by the same staring eyes as she overtook; the grey little girl and the petulant boy leaning on his shovel, wiping his nose on his sleeve as she went by.

The hairs on the back of her neck prickled as both children held her gaze.

Shocked, she forced herself to calm down before in a little while she found a place to stop. Her hosts drummed up a rudimentary evening meal and she settled down to a good night's sleep – for once undisturbed by tortured nightmares of self-recrimination and loathing.

Instead she suffered different dreams – of two macabre children in a horse-drawn cart, pointing at her and laughing cruelly. The little girl was mouthing something...*each breaking dawn.*

Saturday, June 17th

The next morning she settled the bill and was just about to heave her overnight bag out to the car when a minor error on the receipt caught her attention.

"You've written the fifteenth – June the fifteenth," she lightly admonished the landlady, a spritely old widow with striking silver hair. "You're a day or two out. Yesterday was Friday the sixteenth so today must be Saturday the seventeenth."

The woman took the receipt and lowered her spectacles from their perch at the top of her head to read it better. "I'm afraid it's you who's out," she replied patiently. "Today is Thursday. Thursday the 15th. *Tomorrow* is Friday."

Gemma smiled indulgently and didn't press the point. She had paid, that was all that mattered. The old woman was obviously a little batty. She hurried to her car and prepared for another few hours behind the wheel. By late afternoon, she had left the industrial bleakness of Birmingham behind and spotted another reasonable place to stay the night, an ordinary detached bungalow with a faded sign in the front garden promising "Black Country Hospitality".

Gemma booked in and settled down with a hasty plate of sorry looking cheese sandwiches before heading for bed. She awoke refreshed and settled the bill gratefully. One more day in England and then she would be over the border and heading on the last lap for home.

Sunday June 18th/ Wednesday June 14th

As she drove north she pulled into the forecourt of a garage. A friendly man in red, grease-stained overalls passed nearby as she filled up the tank. He had tousled brown hair and a ridiculous one-inch Hitler moustache under a purple blotched nose.

"Those tyres look a little unloved, miss," he remarked casually. "I should top them up if I was you, especially if you're going any distance." His heavy accent was imbued with Brummie/Black Country charm.

She frowned as she cast her eyes over the tiny wheels of her black Mini Cooper. They did look a little flat. "Thank you. Can I inflate them here?"

"Normally, miss. But Jack closes up early on a Wednesday and the stubborn fool won't stump up no tokens after 4pm. No matter – I've a pump round the back in my van. I'll see you safe."

Gemma was grateful as she would never have noticed the tyres, and she decided not to take issue with him over the day. It was Sunday, not Wednesday. Jack should still be handing out the tokens with good grace, but it didn't matter. The mechanic reappeared with a bright red foot-pump barely cleaner than his overalls, and had the job done in a matter of minutes.

"Thank you, sir," she smiled gratefully. "Do I owe you anything?"

He dismissively waved her offer away as he disappeared back behind the garage.

"You've dropped your newspaper," she called out to him, and stepped forward to pick it up. He walked back, raising exasperated eyebrows, and as he did so Gemma caught a glimpse of the front page.

Over the headline *Birmingham Bus Shake-up* she was startled to read that the day really was Wednesday, at least as far as *The Birmingham News and Post* was concerned. *Wednesday, June 14th*.

She struggled to get her head round this. She knew it was Sunday, June eighteenth, two days after leaving Annabelle, but the newspaper clearly thought otherwise.

She handed the paper to the mechanic, her confused thoughts racing. He nodded when she asked if this was that day's paper.

"I know this is a daft question," she said, and squirmed as he cocked an eyebrow in anticipation. His lively, twinkling eyes looked as if they were about to wink at her. "Exactly what day *is* this?"

He grinned with exaggerated forbearance.

"You has been travelling awhile. It's Wednesday, June the …" he paused to check the newspaper dateline. "…fourteenth. You'd best rest up, miss, if you've a way to go yet. No sense in driving while your head's all muggy."

"I'll be… fine," she insisted, as she climbed back into the car.

"Don't think you've paid yet, miss. Jack won't be best pleased. Might set the dogs on you."

"No, of course, silly me," she mumbled, and grabbed her handbag to take to the pay counter. Inside she paid the surly looking man behind the till and, with a glance over her shoulder to ensure the mechanic wasn't within earshot, also asked him what day it was.

"Wednesday. Close early Wednesday," he replied sharply.

She felt dazed as she left, glancing in her mirror to see the worried mechanic scratching his head behind her. Worse, the traffic was heavy and she didn't feel confident in her present state of mind. If it weren't for the wonderful memory of her reunion with her daughter the whole situation would have left her quite depressed. That was the last thing she needed, to go back on those pills. She resolved to make a short day of it and stop over again in an hour or two. Now David had left there was nobody waiting for her at home and Janet next door would continue to feed the cats and the goats without complaint.

So by 6pm she booked into a small comfortable hotel well south of Manchester, ensuring she got a good square meal and lots of rest. On impulse she went to the bar and asked the young barman for a "good stiff drink".

He studied her for a moment and saw before him a woman 'of advancing years' – she was in her late fifties – who might need to keep a clear head for her journey the next day.

"I can rustle you up a mean coffee?" he suggested. "Or a tomato juice positively pulsing with Worcester sauce?"

He had a cheerful round face topped with a head of thinning, wispy hair that looks so unfortunate on the young, like premature ageing. His name was Sam.

"I'll take the latter, please, but with a generous measure of vodka, if you don't mind. I've had a hard day."

"One Bloody Mary coming up," he confirmed, and set to work busily, if a little reluctantly. "Ice?"

She nodded and greedily eyed the fast filling glass. Maybe this would do the trick, she thought.

It wasn't the only one she had that evening, and by ten o' clock she had told Sam all about the reunion she had both dreaded and dreamed of for twenty years, about the shame and the relief. How she had taken all that time to build up the courage to finally tell her daughter she was sorry for the pain her heartlessness had caused.

"When your life is a barren desert just the merest sniff of an oasis on the horizon can turn you into a monster ready and willing to abandon all your responsibilities," she told him. "David burned with the warmth I had been denied so long. You know it's over when you wake up and find a space the size of a Sainsbury's car park between you – and it's not enough! It had been that way with Reg and I for five years, since soon after our daughter was born. David was handsome and exciting and I just couldn't resist him. Unfortunately he wasn't interested in taking on Annabelle and so I went without her. Just like that. One day David and I woke up to find that same car park between us – and he didn't much care for shopping either."

Sam looked thoughtful as he cleaned glasses on the bar.

"It must be a horrible thing for a girl, to have her mother walk out when so young," he remarked, rather undiplomatically, Gemma thought. "Was it David's leaving that finally gave you the strength to look her up?"

"Maybe," she mused. "But I can't really use him as an excuse. I was simply terrified of the consequences. I knew what I had done was unforgivable and I couldn't see anything I could ever do or say would make it up to my deserted daughter."

"But everything's all right now?" he asked.

"Oh yes," said Gemma dreamily. "Everything's perfect. I should have done it years ago but I think it was the coming of the New Millennium that was the spur. A new century – a splendid time to make amends. I found Annabelle's address through old friends – who made it quite plain they thought me an evil witch, incidentally. She didn't even know I was coming – I was lucky to find her at home."

There was an uncomfortable pause.

"Supposed to be all sorts of things happening this New Year's Eve," Sam digressed distractedly. "Computers crashing, planes falling out of the sky, maybe even the end of the world."

"Nothing about time running backwards, I suppose?" She hadn't expected an answer and simply shook her head at his dumb, puzzled reaction.

She'd had a drink or two but found the wit to try a little test.

"Well, I don't know about the end of the world but I do know it's not the end of the road for me. I've got to get an early start in the morning and Monday is likely to be very busy."

"You've had one too many of those Bloody Marys, I'm afraid, Mrs Fairweather. Tomorrow is Thursday not Monday."

Her headache was nothing compared to the migraine when she woke up the next morning to neither a Monday nor a Thursday but to a bright and sunny Tuesday.

Monday June 19th/Tuesday June 13th

"Oh my dear, dear God," she exclaimed in sheer horror, when she saw the date on her complimentary morning paper. "Is this never going to end?"

"Is something the matter, madam?" asked the drably dressed hotelier in a dusty and faded brocade waistcoat.

"What day is it?" asked Gemma, in a small voice.

"Tuesday June the thirteenth," asserted the hotelier cheerfully.

"It can't be! I booked in... last night," she stuttered. "On Sunday, June eighteenth. Either I'm going mad or time is going backwards!"

The hotelier was clearly amused as she paid up and ran from the reception desk like a crazy woman. She could imagine the scene she left behind as the barman and the hotelier stared after their distressed guest.

"Just look at that," the hotelier was probably saying. "One crazy woman."

"She had a skinful last night," Sam would have told him. "Didn't even know what day it was."

"Didn't know what day it was today, either."

She knew she must have looked as wretched as she felt as she threw her bag in the car and took off at high speed.

"...Acting like there's no tomorrow," she could hear them agreeing.

But for Gemma there were no tomorrows – only yesterdays. She tried to come to terms with the reality of what was happening; the days of the week really were in *reverse.*

For the rest of the journey she checked the date en route in restaurants, police stations, at newspaper vendors, even on one occasion at a hospital where she almost booked herself in. But she didn't – she simply asked the puzzled nurses what day it was and fled.

At sunset on the final day, which for her was Tuesday June the twentieth, everyone else went to bed saying their goodbyes to Monday June the twelfth and were busy looking forward to Tuesday June the thirteenth.

But Gemma tossed and turned with the loneliest and scariest secret – grimly aware that when she woke up it would be Sunday, June eleventh, the date she left. She fell into a fitful slumber with an ironic grimace on her lips as she mouthed the phrase, *sure as day.*

Wednesday June 21st/ Sunday June 11th

The next morning she boarded the early ferry from Fort William and drove over the causeway to Eriskay. There was no sign of Janet at her cottage but the animals had evidently been well looked after.

She collapsed with her head in her hands, a ragged, wreck of a woman who had seemingly driven backwards in time for nearly a week. The calendar on her kitchen wall was still ringed at Sunday, June eleventh – the day the nightmare began.

She had been gone ten days – it should now have been Midsummer's Day, Wednesday June twenty-first. But a quick call to the island operator confirmed what her chilled heart already knew.

"It's Sunday, June eleventh, dear. Is there anything I can do for you?"

She was right back precisely where she started.

Her mind could make no sense of anything. She raced upstairs to the bathroom and clumsily turfed out the medicine cabinet looking for the diazepam. She threw half empty bottles of aspirin this way and that but there was none to be found. She had used it all.

Gemma was a quivering mess, sobbing violently in the pitch dark when Janet called in later that night.

"My poor lass," she exclaimed when she turned on the light and saw the quaking wretch on the floor. She knelt down and wrapped her arms around her, dabbing her eyes with a quickly sodden handkerchief.

"What happened to your visit to your daughter? I hope you have nae intention of leaving now. I canna let ye go in this state."

"I have to call Annabelle," whimpered the sad, distraught ruin in her arms. "I have to tell her I arrived home safely. She'll be worried."

A look of even deeper concern clouded Janet's face. "Of course, lass. Now…just take it easy. Janet's going to call Doctor Stuart."

"Fine," said Gemma. "But I must call Annabelle. Her number's on my mobile." She looked around through tear-misted eyes in vain. "I must have left it in the car. It's open – would you be kind enough…?"

"Of course."

Moments later Janet was back with the phone but after fumbling wildly with the buttons Gemma threw it to the floor in frustration.

"I could have sworn I put her number in – but it's just not there."

Once more Janet embraced her. "Gemma, dear. You never left. You haven't been to your daughter's. Please calm down. I'm going to ring the doctor right now – he'll be here in a trice."

Doctor Stuart naturally ordered her straight to bed with a strong sedative and the promise that he would look in every day. Through an exhausted, bleary haze she listened to his soothing assurances and wearily accepted his medical prognosis as she desperately sought the solace of sleep.

Sitting on the edge of her bed with his hand on her brow he told her: "I don't pretend to be a practitioner of psychology but I am aware that you have sought psychiatric help in the past and I know something of your background." He cleared his throat. "The mind is a powerful machine and will protect itself when necessary and I think that is what has happened here. You made up your mind to confront your daughter after all these years and in your mind you *believe* you did. I bet everything went swimmingly, did it not?"

She was hazily aware that the doctor was smiling kindly.

“But I believe your traumatised mind was protecting you from the confrontation you feared more than anything. You *imagined* you went but if you check your vehicle’s mileage when you are up and about again, I think you will see you haven’t really been anywhere. You can’t really have set out this afternoon on the ferry to travel some 1,000 miles or more and been back in time for your tea, now can you?

“The brain is a magnificent, mysterious machine and has invented this scenario to shield you from the trauma it knows you just can’t take. The ‘travelling backwards in time’ illusion was just a way to bring you back to reality.”

Gemma was slipping into an exhausted sleep and missed most of his reassuring, plausible explanation before the release of dreams swept over her. But she heard enough to feel confident that when she woke up it would be tomorrow and not yesterday.

Janet was perfectly willing to look after her while she was under the doctor’s care and immediately set about tidying up downstairs. She was humming to herself as she picked up something small and woollen she had earlier brought in from the car where it had been laying on the backseat next to Gemma’s mobile.

“What a bonny wee toy that is,” she said to herself, as she placed it carefully on the mantelpiece.

It was finger-puppet – a Swiss mountain maid with impossibly rosy red cheeks and a bright blue bonnet.

Did You Mean Bludgeoned?

A shining, golden host of 1,000 gigabyte angels danced merrily about Elliot's spikey, orange hair, sweetly singing pixelated psalms into each of his pierced ears. He was in Hi-Spec heaven!

He adjusted the small, round National Health-style glasses on his rather wizened little face and sat there glowing, the cat who'd got the cream; the cream in this case being a powerful new state-of-the-art pc with knobs on. After all the glitches, frozen screens and interminable drumming of impatient fingers waiting for downloads that never even *pretended* to download, he had finally dumped his 10-year-old machine and bought the ultimate dream-spinner. WiFi, DVD, Blu Ray… wondrous terms his mates smugly spouted non-stop called to him from an Aladdin's Cave of technological temptation.

He leaned back, hands behind his head, and sighed deep with satisfaction. Now he wouldn't have to keep apologising each time he tried to send Sammy one of his homemade keyboard tracks which invariably failed to materialise at Sammy's end. Neither would he have to hang his head in shame as he explained to Aunt Beth in Melbourne that the latest family photo had left the white cliffs of England's air space alive and well.

"Must have got swallowed up in the ether," he would shrug on Skype, embarrassed.

His own niece had scoffed that nobody of her generation would even recognise his wind-up, clockwork contraption as a computer.

But now he could walk proud among his pals and, who knows, soon be swapping stories about how he had hacked into Kazakhstan's defence system (if they even have one) or *precisely* computed the *exact* number of habitable planets out there in the great wide universe. Sitting there just waiting for civilisation and their very own McDonalds.

He leaned forward and opened Google, ready for his first interaction with the Silver God at his fingertips. He frowned as he saw something already written in the search bar.

"Bit weird," he thought and grumpily deleted it before inserting *CAN QPR BE SAVED FROM RELEGATION?* Soccer was a burning passion and he spent a somewhat depressing hour summing up his favourite team's hopes for the next Cup before signing off for lunch. As a QPR fan like his father before him, he heated his Thai curry with a dejected lack of enthusiasm, but then remembering he was the owner of a brand new 21st century computer he woofed it down a little more heartily.

Breaking off another generous length of French baguette Elliot started thinking about how his search engine could have come to him already primed with a subject request. What was it again? Horswick Chapel. That was it. Peculiar. He made a mental note to ask the supplier about it. It should have been removed even if it was a test search.

Later that day he was once again at his desk and after some exploratory examination of the simpler programmes decided to look up the benefits of Blu Ray. Up came the search bar and to his astonishment there it was again… *HORSWICK CHAPEL.* And he hadn't even touched the keyboard!

Bewildered but curious, he pressed *search.* There were six entries, none remotely interesting. A picture of an old chapel on a Lake District hill stared out at him, cold, lonely and windswept. Was there something familiar about it? Its walls were nothing more than a memory although two windows were still just about worthy of the name. Last inhabited by Franciscan friars centuries ago, he read with very little interest. Famous locally for their wine. Good for them. Nothing like a tot or two of the hard stuff to brighten up confession time to The Boss. The chapel was all that was left of what was once a sprawling monastery.

With a dismissive grunt he scrubbed the words from the search bar and set about the task in hand, the wonders of Blu Ray.

It was nearly midnight before he finished playing with his new toy, by which time he had told every one of his fifteen Facebook pals about his new Super Machine.

"Now you can keep bang up to date with QPR's triumphs," one pal quipped. "Guess you'll be in counselling soon."

As he prepared to switch off he found himself again looking at the default search page and there it was, back again: *HORSWICK CHAPEL.*

“What the hell?” he grumbled, as he deleted the line and then sat back and watched the blank search bar. After a few seconds it reappeared. He repeated this ritual several times in a row – delete, wait… delete, wait. Horswick Chapel seemed determined to haunt him until either the system crashed or his brain did.

Resolute, he rebooted the machine.

HORSWICK CHAPEL.

He hit ‘help’, read about browser caches. Feeling very well informed and wise, he then cleared his history, deleted his cookies, switched off, unplugged the electrics and waited an hour before again rebooting.

HORSWICK CHAPEL.

He finally gave up and crawled to bed but didn’t sleep for long, his dreams taking him to a chapel ruin on a bleak hillside. There was an oppressive, brooding atmosphere about the place and he was leaning on a twisted, gnarled tree when a rising icy wind made him shiver. He woke up in a cold sweat, trying desperately to remember the tiniest details. There had been something on the ground near the broken walls, an object. But he couldn’t quite remember what it was. Resigned to a broken night, he threw on his dressing gown and padded downstairs for a hot chocolate to help him relax. Returning to bed he felt compelled to enter his study and sit down at the desk. For a few moments he did nothing but sip at his drink, then leaned forward and switched everything on. There was a satisfyingly soft whirr and a buzz and within seconds the screen burst into life. He opened the browser and sat back, resigned.

HORSWICK CHAPEL.

But this time there was something else… the letters SE – *HORSWICK CHAPEL. SE.* His fever forgotten, his brow furrowed to a frown.

“It’s a flamin’ treasure hunt,” he said out loud. “South east? South east of the chapel?”

It was very late, a little after four by his watch, and he could feel the hairs prickle on his neck. For the first time, he wished he didn’t live alone. With his admittedly strange looks, he had never considered himself boyfriend material, and neither unfortunately did girls. He wasn’t sufficiently interested in the physical side of life to romance with much gusto. He once flirted briefly on a dating site stipulating: *A passion for sport and a sense of humour essential but sex not important*. He quit when three of the five replies came from men.

As he was musing on the downside of bachelorhood things got even spookier. The requested search subject vanished and was immediately replaced with another word: *BLUGGEONED*.

He selected *Enter* and smiled grimly when asked on-screen: *DID YOU MEAN: BLUDGEONED?* Pressing bravely on he was treated to gory descriptions he could well have done without, sitting alone in his house in the middle of the night. His body gave an involuntary shudder, and he switched off and went to bed.

The next day he awoke calm and strangely resolute. It was a holiday and he didn't have to be back at work for several days – he was under-manager at a dairy not far from Manchester. He packed a bag and set off for the Lake District.

Soon enough he was hunting for the hilltop with the chapel ruin and was surprised how long it took him to find it. Eventually, with the guidance of a passing shepherd he parked his car and climbed the bleak hillside of his dark dream. On his back were a few implements he thought he might need. And suddenly there it was – Horswick chapel!

Just like the picture he had already seen, there was little of interest. A low, twisted tree stood a few yards off from the ruin, and the wind whistled eerily, chilling his soul. But again came that vague feeling of déja vu. Had he played here as a child? It was quite possible. Several family holidays had been spent in the Lakes. Was this why he had been singled out for the messages – did he have some sort of subconscious affinity with the spot? Anyway, there was work to be done. With his compass he located the south east corner of the chapel. The earth was soft enough, although riddled with big stones, and in two hours he had dug an area big enough to locate a shallow grave. Nothing. No Franciscan monk, bludgeoned or otherwise. For the first time that day he felt totally foolish and fervently hoped nobody would chance upon his evil deeds. It was summer, although you'd never know it from the weather, and the chances of walkers coming this way were high. He looked awkwardly around him, as sly and sheepish as a graverobber.

After a few minutes rest, he put the spade to work again filling in the hole he had made. The cool afternoon was drawing to a close when he had finished, carefully rectifying the disturbed surface with grass turfs.

Disappointed, he packed his bag and was about to set off back down the hill when he remembered his dream. There was an object. He couldn't tell what it was but with a little thought he believed he could work out *where* it was.

He stood a few paces back from the anarchic chaos of fallen stones and stroked his chin. Yes, he was confident he had it. He located the spot as precisely as he could and stared at the ground, about three yards from the middle of the west wall. If only he could decipher what it was he thought he'd seen. He closed his eyes to concentrate and tried to envisage the scene exactly as he had in his sleep the previous night.

A hammer! It had been a hammer.

Quickly, for the light would soon be fading, he once again took out his shovel and started to dig frantically, convinced this time he was where X marked the spot.

Within an hour he struck something creepily unnatural. At first he thought it was just another hard clod of earth that gave under pressure. But as his spade sank, so did his nauseated senses. He just *knew* this was human flesh and bone.

An early twilight was falling in the misty hills and he stared agog at what he had found – the decomposing body of a man dressed, not as a monk, but in modern clothes. He could make out the dirt-encrusted weave of a pullover and trouser shreds loosely clinging to the sickening remains of flesh. Amid the mud, glimpses of off-white bone. There were horrible, messy wounds to the splintered skull and, lying next to the body... a blood-stained hammer.

Elliot just stared at the corpse as one more mystery niggled at his brain. Why had the messages indicated the southeast? This spot was very definitely *west* of the chapel.

"Oi! What do you think you're doing?" The sudden bark of an angry voice shook Elliot's strained nerves and he stumbled, falling straight into the mound of earth he had just created.

He peered through dislodged, mud-clogged specs at a uniformed policeman. Next to him, looking shifty, was another man he recognised. It was the shepherd who had given him directions. He had obviously considered Elliot a suspicious character worth the attention of the local constabulary. Must have been the orange hair, he mused, or maybe the spade handle sticking out from his backpack!

"I think… I think I've found a body," said Elliot, mustering as much dignity as he could as he stood, brushing off his clothes.

Later he learned that the corpse – who after a thorough forensic examination was identified and given a proper burial in a nearby village – was a hapless holidaymaker who disappeared two years earlier in mysterious circumstances. He had been walking these hills but nobody knew exactly where he took his last steps. Last seen in Keswick some four miles away, he had attracted unwanted attention in a pub by buying several rounds of drinks for the locals.

"Brought it upon himself, he did," said the policeman after the story had been revealed. "Bit of a thicko throwing his money around like that. Someone followed him with an 'ammer in his pocket. Lonely spot, that hill. Nobody was ever likely to find 'im."

Elliot kept quiet about how exactly he had come to be digging for dead bodies on this remote hillside. He mumbled something about an archaeological dig and strangely, nobody seemed much bothered.

When he got home he found just one final message on his computer. It read: *PEECE AT LAST. THANK YOU. SE.*

Elliot put his feet up on the desk and stared at the screen, a hint of a grim smile on his lips. Stuart Edwards would never have won a prize for spelling but he had to concede his communication skills were out of this world.

Dining by Moonlight

After the full moon, came the snow. The garden under its thick white blanket looked like a macabre but stunningly beautiful stage set. Familiar landmarks were reborn into something brand new and exciting; that old wooden bench by the back wall of the terrace morphed into a sumptuous sofa, generously upholstered by four inches of snow. And the wall itself, looking more like the side of a tantalising, giant Christmas cake, topped with an extravagant layer of mouth watering icing sugar. Bushes, trees and plants that had been there for years were suddenly transformed into weird and wonderful Jurassic shapes. The snow clung to each branch and leaf as if it had been forever thus. The sky, steady black, lorded over that mysterious, muffled silence that only mid-winter snow can bring.

I had been keeping my nightly vigil since 8.30pm. It was now 11.45 and I knew it was now or never. My dinner guest was a fickle creature who liked his sleep. If he didn't come by midnight, he wouldn't show at all. Sometimes he didn't. Sometimes he had something better to do, someone more interesting to visit. I prepared to return to my bed, disappointed.

But then I saw it, an unmistakeable glint of absurdly bright ginger, skulking out of the bushes at the far end of the garden. He looked at the house and I felt sure he knew I was watching. He stood, one paw partly raised, like a stalking cat. I could see the frost on his whiskers even from 120 feet away. The snow, disturbed from the bushes of his hiding place, gently showered onto his long, sleek back like ice-cold confetti.

At last, reassured, the handsome fox edged forward towards my nightly offering, his black nose twitching in anticipation. I had boiled the meat from the bone, and it sat there, a tempting feast, lightly sprinkled by an earlier flurry of snow. The fox set its belly down and sprawled carelessly before the banquet, his head twisting from side to side as he chewed in the bright moonlight.

Fiona loved the big ginger fox. Fergus, she called him. Furry Fergus. Sometimes when we stood at this window together I could feel her chest heave with palpable excitement when he at last crept stealthily into view. She would clasp her hands together and exclaim something sweet and facile, sounding like a two-year-old seeing the Christmas tree for the first time.

I smiled now as I watched Fergus hungrily enjoy his supper. It was as if Fiona was still by my side and I could imagine her clinging to my dressing gown in her innocent enthusiasm.

"Oh, what a handsome creature," she would say. "I wish – how I wish – we could have him as a pet."

"You can't domesticate a full-grown fox," I would tell her. But she knew that. She knew that, but it didn't stop her dreaming.

With a sigh, I turned reluctantly from the scene and went to bed.

The next night I was there again at the window, 8.15pm prompt, waiting for the curtain to rise. The snow was still thick on the ground but, without the reinforcements of fresh falls, it had lost its pure lustre. Yet the scene in the garden was still spectacularly backlit by the waning moon, and I shivered once more with that unmistakable anticipation as if I were sitting in the Royal Circle, my programme in my lap.

He came earlier this time, emerging from the same clump of bushes near the greenhouse. Again the small splatter of snow on his back from the disturbed branches. I smiled at myself as I realized I had taken a sharp intake of breath as soon as I had spotted him.

"See, Fiona, you're not the only one whose heart is stirred by the ginger fox."

I was talking to myself, naturally. But it was easy to picture her still standing by my side at the window. Easy to remember her child-like thrill whenever that sleek, marmalade coat came into view. I could see her now, fingers excitedly interlocked with some sort of deep yearning for the mystery of a creature she could not possess, the call of the wild reaching out to a part of her I could not touch. He sang to the feral in her. He'd been coming for more than a year now, our own midnight caller. He had never been so well fed.

"Oh Mr Fox what big teeth you've got," I mouthed slowly and clearly, as I watched him chewing his bloody feast, my breath misting up the window pane inches from my face. With my finger I traced the words "Fi 4 Fergus" on the glass.

My body shivered with the sudden chill of the night and I hugged my dressing gown more tightly around me. It was only

9.30pm but already I yearned for the warmth and comfort of my bed. No Fiona to keep me warm now, just her old pink hot water bottle on my feet. An old pink hot water bottle and sheets still warm and scented from the memory of her.

Again I sighed, as I took a last look at the fox down on his haunches, oblivious to everything but his generous supper, and then I retired to the bedroom.

The next night he didn't show until 11.30pm. But again he seemed to gaze long and hard at the house as he came out from the bushes, and I wondered if he knew that this was where his nightly treat came from. Was that gratitude I could detect in his bright brown eyes as he edged closer to his waiting meal? I laughed out loud at my own silliness and stood a while longer watching him before finally turning in, satisfied. We would both sleep soundly tonight, he with his full stomach and me with a contented heart.

As I pulled the blanket right up under my chin and reached to turn out the lamp I was still thinking about Fergus, his slinky ginger coat flecked with specks of snow as he ravenously ate his fill. He might have been beautiful, but his table manners left a lot to be desired. No wonder he always dined alone.

"You've had it easy so far," I whispered out loud. "I've been boiling the meat off the bone for you.

"Tomorrow I'm going to try you with her head. See how you get on with that."

Heavenbound

“Starting countdown: Engines on...” The whole world stopped breathing as the giant silver spaceship started to take on an awesome, unstoppable life of its own.

“Ten... nine... eight... seven...”

Bailey scanned his instrument panel and prepared himself for launch. He had done this many times before, in simulation and for real, but could never entirely shake off those fluttering nerves that attacked his belly like a storm of butterflies.

“… six ... five... four... three... two.... one... lift off!”

The power surged through him like a never-ending earthquake, a rumbling sensation that set every tiny nerve on fire. He never felt more alive nor so near his certain demise. *Pegasus IV* roared into the skies in an ecstasy of perpetual slow motion.

“OK fellah, Code Green. Everything AOK! You’re *heavenbound*.”

Bailey’s first reply avoided the temptation to lapse into homely humour, a natural and ubiquitous release mechanism for all that tension. The atmosphere both at Houston Control and in the ship is stretched taut prior to a new launch. It is never routine.

“Check that,” he said. And then added: “Baby’s on the road.”

An hour later he had completed his inventory and had mentally ticked every box. Now it was time to settle down for his semi-hibernatory sleep which would see him through his four-day voyage among the stars to Astion 1, the new moon discovered by chance from an observatory in Hawaii.

He reached with his tongue to gently puncture the rice-paper pouch on the inside of his helmet and swallowed the soft, gelatine lozenges lodged there. This would provide enough sustenance for his entire journey and he would automatically wake refreshed in good time for landing.

“Goodnight Houston. Permission to go shuteye?”

“Permission granted, Pegasus. Sweet dreams.”

When man first journeyed to the moon in 1969 it took him two days to blaze his pioneering pathway across 250,000 miles of empty, black space. But Bailey had been born in the age of advanced quantum physics and two days space travel would take a man considerably farther than the earth's moon. Light years, in fact. It was 2050 and when he awoke he was in one of the furthest reaches of outer space detectable with the latest state-of-the-art telescope technology.

He was instantly alert, his mind immediately ready for the tasks before him. He checked his read-outs and acknowledged Houston's request for a journey's-end update.

"Everything AOK," said Bailey. "Astion 1 beckoning like a hungry baby below."

"OK," barked the radio. "Let infant see Mama's bottle."

He set the auto switches and laboriously shifted from his comfortable, all embracing cockpit chair to negotiate the four feet to the entrance of the Lander.

A tethered screen pen floated harmlessly into his face during his semi-glide to the other side of the cockpit, and in slow motion he raised his right arm to brush it away.

Within seconds he had unlocked the circular titanium mechanism which gave him entrance to the Lander. He climbed slowly, clumsily inside, looking more like a ballet dancer encumbered by a ring of white car tyres than an astronaut.

There was a 'shooshing' noise as the door locked itself behind him and after a brief session of button pushing he heard the same, strangely comforting sound again as the Lander slipped effortlessly from the mothership to begin its descent.

He entered an even more silent, embryonic world than the one that had nurtured him for the past 96 hours.

He was never entirely happy in the Lander. He could sense the same uncomfortable stirrings of claustrophobia that he always felt on planet landings. It was a necessary evil that rarely lasted more than 45 minutes, to be endured silently and without complaint. But, sure enough, here it came again – a flash of some by now almost familiar nightmare momentarily invading his brain like forked lightning. *An impending collision, panic, heart-breaking panic, and a cacophony of noise followed by an overwhelming sense of loss.* This was a vision he would be sure *not* to mention to the team psychiatrist. He knew he would be ordered to rest and sent off-duty for God knows how long. But it was soon over and he put it down to the extra stress inside the loathed Lander.

It wasn't long before the Lander was reverse-thrusting against the green landscape, Bailey's temporary discomfort forgotten as he marvelled at the sight before him. Astion 1 was an anomaly. It shouldn't have been there in the first place and had remained undetected through decades of sweeps by advanced space monitoring technology.

Baffled scientists had speculated that it had hitherto been masked by a peculiar astral gas cloud that permanently bathed Spectre, the earth-sized planet Astion 1 orbited.

Bailey was almost breathless, gazing upon its beauty as the Lander set down in a lush green meadow of disquietingly familiar yellow and white flowers.

"Houston, I'm stepping out," he breathed into his headset radio as the door shooshed outwards.

"Roger that," came the reply. "Be careful now. It may be a jungle out there."

"A jungle it most certainly isn't," whispered Bailey, more to himself than to Control, as he stepped out onto the soft, damp grass.

He knew at once there was oxygen here and that he would be able to breathe as naturally as he could on earth.

"All readings normal. Non-toxic atmosphere. Oxygen and gravity all pretty much earthlike," he reported. "I am going to remove my helmet."

He ignored the spluttered warnings coming tinnily from the headphone as he removed the helmet and hungrily breathed the sweet, scented air.

He fought back a tear as he turned to face the meadow stretching gently away uphill from him, towards a hedgerow ridge at the top. Nostalgia swamped him as he thought first of his childhood home on England's Sussex Downs and then of his father and mother who still lived there.

As he gazed across the blanket of grass wafting dreamily in the breeze, and mottled with buttercups, daisies and clover, he pictured his dad pottering about in his garden at home. He would be constantly checking his wristwatch, desperate not to miss a single TV or radio broadcast that might offer up some news of his son's space-shot. And he thought of his mother, too, wiping her hands on a kitchen apron as she perched on the arm of Dad's chair, also eager to catch any snippet of news.

How he loved them, even though that love was tinged with regret as he considered how they hid their disappointment that he never married to give them the grandchildren they so yearned for.

They were too set in their ways to relocate to America and, besides, they would have missed their home on the Sussex Downs too much. But he realized he had let them down by not finding a wife. He had had girlfriends but he was too absorbed in his career among the stars to be tied down to any kind of domestic routine, although many of his American colleagues at the Nasa space station in Florida did manage to juggle duty with diapers.

But it wasn't for him.

On impulse, although it was strictly against the rulebook, Bailey hastened out of his spacesuit and strolled back to the Lander to stow it safely until his return.

Gravity was definitely a 'g' or two less here, he noted mentally, for entry in the log later; he seemed to have the nimble step of a young lamb.

He stepped back from the Lander and pressed the remote control that would protect it in his absence behind an invisible shield. Then he turned and purposefully strode up the slope towards the ridge.

As he neared the top, his heart lightened even more as he heard the sound of birdsong. The sound was as English as any Sussex garden. Finally he stood in a natural gap in the hedgerow to gaze down on the meadow falling gently away the other side.

Not 100 yards from where he stood he could see a wooden house, reminiscent of the American deep south, and an old man – totally *human* – puffing on a pipe as he relaxed in a rocking chair on the front porch.

The man noticed him almost at once and hailed him with a wave and a friendly shout. Bailey hastened towards him, not considering for one moment there could be any danger.

As he approached the old man, who was dressed in a comfortable white open shirt and dark blue jeans, he was stunned to hear himself being addressed in English.

"Hi there, son. You must be new around here."

"I'm an astronaut," began Bailey lamely. "I've just arrived from earth. You know where earth is?"

The old man's eyes were laughing as he said: "Oh yes. I know where earth is. But you must be hungry. Fancy some milk and cookies?"

Bailey was dumbstruck. He couldn't believe that this old man seemed to be laughing at him.

"The name's Bailey. Captain John Bailey of the USAF space centre." He held out his hand, which the old man took and shook warmly.

"Well, welcome to my shack, Captain. Mind if I call you Johnny?" He turned sideways to indicate to Bailey that he should step forward and go inside, which he did, in a kind of daze.

They sat at a pine table while the old man poured milk into a tumbler and produced some biscuits on a plate.

"These are good. We make 'em ourselves," he said, and commenced to chatter on about this and that as if he met an astronaut from earth every day.

Presently they were joined by a young girl of about 14 who sat down shyly at the table and commenced to study Bailey with intense interest.

"This is my daughter Emma," the man said kindly. "Say hello to Captain John Bailey, an astronaut from earth." Again, his eyes sparkled.

He *is* laughing at me, Bailey thought, unnerved.

"Hello," said Emma, and continued to stare at Bailey while the old man nattered on about their lives on the small dairy farm they ran together.

Eventually, the old man seemed to be struck by an idea. "Why don't you show Johnny around the place, Emma?"

At once her eyes sprang alive and she rather too eagerly leapt out of her seat to grab Bailey's hand, urging him to follow her. He obliged and turned to study the old man's face as he was tugged towards a back door.

"Have a good time," he said. "Don't be too long and I'll fix up a spot of dinner for us all."

Emma excitedly dragged Bailey out into the sunlight and, where she had been silent before, now she couldn't stop chatting.

"We have chickens, sheep and cows and horses," she went on. "Everything we want – right here."

"You understand I am from earth?" he stammered, and was even more alarmed when the idea seemed to inspire a fit of giggles in the young girl.

"Of course you are," she said, sweetly enough. "Want to see my secret place?"

At this she continued to pull him with both hands towards a nearby barn, open at the front and with bales of straw stacked untidily either side of the entrance.

Bailey was aware that she had been flirting with him and he was afraid of hurting her feelings with a rebuff. As she almost literally pulled him inside the shady barn he became even more concerned.

"Up there," she said, rather more quietly, conspiratorially, and gestured towards a barn ladder leaning up against the stacked hay on a second level. "It's my very own secret place. Want to see?"

She had edged uncomfortably close. This was a situation Bailey wanted to extricate himself from, fast.

"Look," he began. "I think we should get back to your father..." But even as he began, Emma had closed in on him in the murky gloom of the barn and kissed him full on the lips, resisting his attempts to push her away.

"Emma, no..." he shouted, and turned towards the sunlight of the barn door as if for assistance. He was at once horrified and relieved to see the old man standing there, meditatively puffing on his pipe.

"Don't mind me," he chuckled. "Give her a kiss if you want."

Bailey was shocked. What kind of satanic world had he landed on? Far from being angry, this wretch was actually encouraging him – a 35 year old, a mature adult – to kiss his young daughter. Bailey wrenched himself free of Emma's arms and jostled past the stunned old man to flee down the slope as far from the farm as he could run. He ignored Emma's shouted appeals behind him and didn't stop running until he came across a small hamlet, perhaps a full mile and a half further on.

He came to a halt by a wooden shed at the edge of a clutch of cottages. He leaned over, resting his arms on his knees, fighting to get his breath back. The sweat poured off his brow.

"Hello sonny. You've been running some," said a kindly voice before him. He looked up to see an elderly man and his wife arm in arm just six feet away. It was the woman who had spoken.

“Why don’t you come inside and catch your breath?” The woman had a motherly, sensitive face and Bailey didn’t resist as she put her arm around his shoulders and led him back towards her house. Bailey was struck by the mix of architecture. The old man’s farm had looked like something straight out of the Old West but this looked more like his idea of a Slavic village. As they headed for the couple’s home they passed a water pump and a hay wagon which tilted at an angle, one wheel hanging half off. He was reminded somehow of the Amish homesteads he had heard of in the Mid-West.

Once inside, he was sat down at a table and offered a soft drink and biscuits. God, did these people think he was a child? The events of the last hour had demanded more energy than he’d realised, and he slumped at the table, his head in his hands.

“That’s right, dear,” said the old lady. “You take it easy. I know somebody who will want to speak with you.” She disappeared from the room. The old man continued to smile at him but mercifully let him sit in peace and in silence.

Bailey, head slumped onto his outstretched arm, fell instantly asleep.

Some time later he awoke to find himself in a comfortable bed covered with a patchwork quilt. He was horrified to discover he was naked, and felt only slightly better when he noticed his clothes carefully folded over a hardback cane chair alongside the bed. A jug of water stood by an old fashioned bowl on a bedside table.

This, he thought, was clearly an alien civilisation that mirrored life on earth as it was a couple of hundred years ago. Why, he didn’t know. He lay there quite peacefully, strangely unmoved to make contact with Houston as regulations required. Despite the bizarre incident with Emma up at the farm, he felt peculiarly at home. Through a small, leaded glass window, he could see the blue sky and wisps of white cloud gently nudging each other.

Yes, home, he mused.

After a while he rose, dressed and rinsed his face in the basin. He climbed down the narrow, wooden stairs to the small parlour. The old man and his wife were there, seated at the table, eating a handsome and inviting breakfast.

“Have I slept all night?” he asked, astounded.

"You certainly have, my pet," said the old lady, and the old man smiled but stayed silent beside her. "You obviously needed it. Come and eat."

He took a seat and helped himself to the bread and jam set before him. It was the sweetest tasting feast he had ever known.

"Coffee, dear?"

He nodded and the old lady busied herself at her worktop pouring him a cup. "There's someone coming to see you. They are looking forward to it. We'll take you down to the station when you've finished."

Bailey assumed he was to be introduced to some figure of authority, an elder, and mentally he began preparing his speech. He didn't want to give the wrong impression as he so obviously had done at the farm.

A little later, they all stepped out into the warm sunshine and for the first time Bailey noticed a motor car. In fact, two. One was old like a motor museum relic and the other was much more modern, but of a type he couldn't recognise. Naturally enough, he reasoned.

But what struck him as completely odd was that neither vehicle made any sort of noise as it traversed the dusty, unmade streets of the village. They looked like the internal combustion or electric engine powered vehicles of his youth, but operated in total, eerie silence.

Bailey's head was full of his prepared speech for the imminent meeting, so he kept his thoughts to himself. He decided he couldn't take too much on board at any one time.

They walked briskly through the lanes, through a picture postcard world long since defunct back home, until they came to the white picket fence of what was apparently a railway station. *Tweezledown Halt*, the sign on the platform read. Was he in some sort of theme park?

The three of them stood expectantly on the platform and Bailey waited for the deep rumble of what had to be a steam train.

But none came. It was true, the big lumbering puffing Billy coming up the line towards them *looked* as if it should be accompanied by all the wheezing, chuffing and clattering normally associated with such ancient engines.

But, despite a thin stream of white smoke coming from its stack, the train pulled into the station as silently as a ghost.

"Electric?" ventured Bailey to his companions.

“No dear. Not electric,” was the only reply – evasive perhaps, but delivered kindly.

At last the train stretched full length along the platform. Bailey looked this way and that, but if he was looking for a mayoral figure in a gold chain, he was disappointed.

“There!” said the woman, pointing to a rear coach out of which climbed two very ordinary looking people. A man and a woman – his mother and his father. He felt sick. He knew this had to be some kind of trickery. But... there they were.

They approached him, smiling, and for a moment nobody seemed to know what to do. Finally his mother stepped forward and took him in her arms. All his adult training told him not to respond but respond he did and they were instantly in torrents of tears.

“Johnny, Johnny, Johnny,” breathed his mother.

“What the hell is happening, Mum?” Bailey was shaking like a leaf as he clasped first his mother and then his father as tightly as he could. “Where are we? I arrived here from earth yesterday after a 96-hour journey through space – how could you possibly be here too? Is it a dream? Am I dreaming?”

“You’re not dreaming, son,” said his father, and Bailey noticed an unnervingly concerned smile on his mother’s lips. He knew that smile and with a growing chill that began somewhere deep inside he began to wish he *was* just dreaming.

“But... I’ve just arrived here by spaceship, to a place never before detected by man. Where is it? Where are we?”

He sensed the reluctance to explain and followed obediently as, without another word, the party of four walked through the strangely old fashioned streets back to the house. Inside, Bailey’s mother said to the old lady: “Do you have a mirror downstairs?”

“There’s a full length dressing mirror through there,” came the reply, and she nodded towards a door set to one side of the stone fireplace.

Bailey’s mother put her arm around him and led him into the room to the mirror. “What do you see?” she said, as they stood together in front of it. His father waited at the doorway.

“Jesus,” screamed Bailey. “I must have gone through some sort of space time continuum! This just can’t be!”

Before him he saw an image of a 15-year-old boy, his face exactly as he remembered it from the old family photographs.

“I’m going crazy,” he bellowed, and tore past his mother and out of the house.

He'd had enough. He hurtled full pelt back towards where he had left the Lander. He gave the farm as wide a berth as possible, heading straight on down the hill the other side of the ridge.

But even as he ran across the sweet, damp grass that had so impressed him the day before, his worst fears were realized. The Lander had gone. There was no trace of it.

“It’s impossible,” he panted out loud. “Nobody could penetrate the protection shield. No force on earth could break through that...” Even in the present bizarre circumstances he couldn’t prevent a wry smile at what he had said.

Behind him he could hear, not an engine, but the soft closing of car doors. He turned to see his mother and father striding towards him.

“Johnny... wait,” implored his mother. He allowed himself to be wrapped once more in her maternal embrace.

“Don’t you remember? Don’t you remember anything?” she implored.

He shook his head dumbly. He was too emotionally exhausted to think.

“There never was a spaceship, Johnny,” she went on. “It was all in your imagination. You always wanted to be a spaceman since you were seven years old...”

“But...” he began, and she held a finger to her lips to urge him to be quiet and listen.

“Don’t you remember what happened? Your Dad and I were taking you to the country fair on the Downs. We were in the car. There was... a terrible accident.”

His brain lurched and his heart missed a beat... *An impending collision, panic, heart-breaking panic, and a cacophony of noise followed by an overwhelming sense of loss.*

Slowly, the grim, unwelcome memory crawled back.

“I saw the car coming – I knew we were going to crash,” he whispered to his mother, trembling with the reborn horror. “So where are we now? What is this place?”

His mother looked at his father as if for support. “We’re safe now,” she said. “We’re together and we’re safe.”

Presumed Dad

She awoke suddenly, heart beating wildly, to the slightest of sounds from the open window near the end of the bed. Her chest pounded, blood thundering through vein and temple as she tightly clasped her rag doll Mindy. Against the dense pre-dawn sky beyond the sash pane, she began to discern a strange black shape in her room, apparently staring at her.

"Hush now," a low, placatory voice implored, its source edging slowly towards the bed, though strangely without menace, as if it were the most natural thing in the world. "I'll not harm you."

Jenny sat bolt upright, her brow in a cold sweat, but somehow she just could not bring herself to scream. She instinctively craved for the figure to come closer, so she could be sure. As she acclimatised to the dark she found herself peering into two unthreatening eyes, even more startled than her own.

"*Daddy*?" she asked simply, as if this wasn't the face she had yearned to see for more than half her life.

In the shifting dimness he was almost exactly how she'd imagined. A tall, handsome prince with the kindly, sympathetic features she could always conjure; not as skinny as Mummy said he'd be, nor as lean as she remembered from the photographs, the batsman in ungainly white shin-pads or proud-to-bursting bridegroom smiling into his bride's lace-veiled face. Gone too was the rakish RAF-style moustache. It was a long time since those pictures had been brought down from their hiding place on top of the wardrobe. It was 1946 and the war had been over for a year but he had never come back. He never would, Mummy had quietly pronounced, eyes brimming with tears. That's why she could no longer bear to rummage through the faded black and white photographs. But Jenny knew she wouldn't have to wait for that old cardboard suitcase to be brought down again before they'd see him. She'd always known it.

"Hello Daddy," she whispered, and smiled shyly as he put a nicotined finger to his lips as a gentle but firm 'shush'.

She wriggled excitedly in her bedclothes and, hugging the blankets close she rose to her knees, the better to stare at the man she hadn't seen for six years, since before she was even five years old.

"Mummy said you'd gone for ever – but I always knew you'd be here one day."

He smiled sadly, his big greatcoat hanging from his shoulders like so many she had seen on weary, demobbed soldiers – other people's fathers.

"Shhh," he urged again. "If you stay still and quiet like a good girl I'll tell you a story."

Jenny thrilled to the deep resonance of his voice, not quite the fun-loving, good-humoured melody she heard every night in her dreams but war was no jolly jape, Mummy had said, and soldiers had to harden themselves as a defence. Obviously they would sound different too.

"Oh please," pleaded Jenny, clutching the blankets around her even tighter, perhaps to compensate for her daddy's peculiar reluctance to hug her. "I'd like that. Did you *used* to tell me stories?"

"Naturally," he asserted in a hoarse whisper, removing a golliwog from a hard chair next to Jenny's bed to make room for his big frame. "Every dad tells stories."

"Oh Daddy, did you miss us?"

"Of course, I did… *Jennifer*," he said and she giggled as she realized he was reading her name, which was stitched all over her pyjamas in pink and blue. "You'll never know…"

"And Mummy?"

"Yes, of course. And Mummy."

"And George?"

"Yes, and George." He looked around the room, a little questioningly. "Where is George?"

"He sleeps in with Mummy."

"Your brother sleeps with Mummy?"

It was Jenny's turn to look perplexed. "George is our cat."

"The cat, of course," he said, and forlornly rubbed his forehead with his right hand. "The war… you know."

"I know," Jenny assured him as gently as she could. She had heard all about shell-shocked invalids limping home from the front. "Red beans and blue jokes the only respite from bombs and bullets… Mummy said that. Blue means dirty." She reached out but couldn't get a grip on the rough material of his coat. It smelled not unpleasantly of tobacco and the cool, night air. She never recalled him smoking. War obviously took a terrible toll.

"We cried and cried," she went on, soothingly. "Then we got a telegram saying you were 'Missing in Action'. Mummy hugged me and we wept until we were exhausted. I tried to read the rest of the telegram but she wouldn't let me, snatching it away. I think it said *Missing in Action, presumed Dad.* So they didn't even really know it was you, did they? That's what 'presumed' means, doesn't it?"

"Yes, it does," he said, and raised his sad eyes to hers. "It was bedlam. They didn't know Jack –" His empty expression hid a dark, disturbing horror.

"The church held a special service, a 'Mumorial' Mummy called it. She smiled when I said it should be a 'Dadorial'. It was nice to see her like that, so I kept saying it. She doesn't smile any more, not that 'real' kind when you know she's happy. She was dressed all in black but I was allowed to wear what I liked so I wore the summer frock you loved. It was a few sizes too small but I *had* to wear it because it was your favourite. Do you remember?"

He stroked his chin, thinking hard. "The pretty pink one?"

"Oh daddy, you *do* remember! And the animals around the hem?"

"Elephants?"

"Baby calves."

"Yes, of course. Calves. *Let's keep our voices down.*"

"After the telegram Mummy said we had to get used to lonely *few chores* or something. But we'd always have each other and you'd still be there, in our hearts. Only I knew one day you'd come home, when you got bored with the war. I knew the war couldn't have been all that exciting even though the newspapers were full of it, like it was some giant game."

"No, it was no game, Jennifer."

"Jenny," she admonished, slightly cross. "Anyway, see that piggy bank over there on my dressing table, next to the one-eyed teddy?"

In the growing light of early dawn he could just make out the tubby porcelain piglet with a pink bow around its neck and another on its curly tail.

"Nearly four whole pounds in there. I've been saving up to take Mummy on a lovely holiday. Every night I check how much I've got – there's a secret opening in his underbelly that you have to unscrew."

"Nifty thrifty," he said, impressed.

"No, a nifty three pounds, fourteen shillings and sixpence three farthings," she retorted, rather too sharply. "Nowhere near nifty fifty yet."

He grinned and stood to lean over her, encouraging her to lay back in her bedclothes. "OK, Jenny. Time for you to get some sleep now otherwise you'll be too tired to have fun tomorrow."

"I sent you my last milk tooth. Mummy gave me an address although she said you might not get it."

"Yes, I got it. Helped keep me safe. Like a talisman."

"Did you carry it always?"

"Yes I did. Everywhere."

"Then you must have it on you now?"

He went very quiet, almost withdrawn.

"Have you? Have you got it on you now?"

"Yes," he said. "I keep it right here, in this tin."

He reached inside his pocket and pulled out a small round tobacco tin with a sailor's head on the lid. On his hat was the name of a ship: *Hero*.

"Was that you, Daddy, a hero?"

"No, not me, Jenny. I was no hero." He made a show of struggling to open the lid and at last passed it to her. "I can't do it – can you?"

She struggled but the lid wouldn't budge. Finally she shook the tin and held it to her ear to see if it rattled.

"There's no noise," she said, disappointed.

"It's wrapped in cotton wool," he explained. "To keep it safe just as it did me."

She shrugged, satisfied, and handed it back to him. "Keep it," she said, at last losing the battle against a sleepy yawn. "Keep it forever."

Reluctantly she nestled in her covers. "It's Saturday. We can play French cricket and rounders with Mummy, like we used to."

"You can play all the games you want… all the games you want."

"And now I don't have to save up all that money, do I? Because you're here – and that's the only treat we ever wanted."

"Blow it all on ice cream and gobstoppers."

"Not allowed gobstoppers," she mumbled drowsily, her voice trailing off to a contented world of garden games with lemonade and watercress sandwiches.

He stood upright, staring down at her, reaching out his hand and smoothing her brow, pushing tiny strands of stray blonde hair from her eyes.

"Sweet dreams," he whispered, but his words were a smokescreen hiding grief and remorse. She was already fast asleep.

As he turned to go, his attention was bushwhacked by the fat pig with pink ribbons around its neck and tail. He used a penny to unscrew the base and silently counted out the takings: three pounds, fourteen shillings and sixpence three farthings. He laid it on the dressing table and stared at it.

Eventually he dug into his pocket and drew out a wad of big white fivers. It had been a good haul that night. He was ashamed.

With an enigmatic sigh he licked his thumb and counted them out on top of Jenny's little pile, a total of eighty three pounds, fourteen shillings and sixpence three farthings.

That'll buy you and your mum a nice break, he thought and silently vowed he would never again do what had been doing.

Then, as the sun began to rise wearily in a cloud-scudded sky, he climbed out stealthy as a cat through the open window. The shadowy figure of another presence in the room, a soldier in a greatcoat and tin helmet, a Lee-Enfield slung across his shoulder, watched his departure. When he had gone, the soldier leaned across the sleeping girl and kissed her cheek. Safe in her deep, dark slumber she sighed and smiled, her eyes tightly closed.

"Goodbye, Daddy," she whispered.

Agua Eterna

March 10th, 1958

They scrambled one by one down the steep, chalky cliff-face, bright blue ropes occasionally snagging on the spiky, dry brush, rocky outcrops hindering their descent into a chasm so deep it had remained a dark secret from mankind for more than a millennia.

Once, without warning, a green and black striped snake fully some four feet long hissed indignantly at the intruders but then meekly retreated to its hole in the crumbly, dry ravine wall.

It took the six of them two hours to traverse the awkward drop of some 500ft, leaving local guides Paco and Javiar at the top in the steaming Venezuelan jungle.

The crampons were difficult to use on the chalky face, and absailing in the intense sticky heat was far from a pleasure. It felt as though they were lowering themselves into the very pit of hell itself.

They had found Professor Jake Henderson's clothes almost by chance at the top of the ravine. An enigmatic, lone wolf of a fellow, in January 1957 he had left his university in Spain, where he lectured on palaeontology and South American history, to go on a mission of his own.

Now, with a mixture of luck and grim determination, the search expedition had traced him to the spot where he had stood for the final time, his clothes piled carefully on top of his rucksack in which they found a note with just one terse, mysterious message: "Home."

At first they thought he must have removed all his clothing – even his hat was atop the sad pile – and wandered off into the dark recesses of the jungle.

But it soon dawned on them that as his belongings were perched just two yards from the cliff edge, he had probably suffered some sort of breakdown and decided in an unhinged moment to plunge naked into the ravine below.

Experienced explorers themselves, they knew better than to wonder what dark thoughts could finally turn a solitary man's mind as he explored the deep Venezuelan jungle totally alone.

At last the team dropped to the gorge basin, and stood on the bed of what had been, millions of years before, a powerful river in an area shown on the map as Yermo, literally uninhabited wasteland. Once the might of this leviathan had churned and carved its way through the terrain, leaving a trail of gorges and canyons. But now it was as dry as dust, tamed by time.

The men prepared themselves for the worst. There was no telling what Henderson's remains would look like after that mighty plunge and months at the mercy of every insect, reptile and bird that would venture this deep on the jungle floor.

Buttressed, they thought, against all possible horrors, they searched until they sighted his bleached skeleton among the white chalky boulders.

He had leapt to his death sure enough, but what they saw cursed them with nightmares for months..

His spread-eagled skeletal remains included not a single broken bone.

His femur had been partially splintered, most likely by a feeding predator, but apart from that every bone was intact – absolutely impossible after such a protracted plunge from the top of the cliff.

"It doesn't make sense," said the team leader, taking off his hat to scratch his head. "He should look like a pile of broken glass shards. It's as if he *glided* all the way down to settle on the bottom like a feather."

February 27th, 1957

There stood before him the most satisfying sight he had ever seen. Dark and mysterious, with wisps of vapour framing the whole, the neverending crescendo of the jungle waterfall threatened to drown him as certainly as plunging into that watery tumult surely would.

He couldn't think through the thunderous noise, but neither could he drag himself away from the mighty glory before him. It was the birth of creation, it was Venus at her most seductive, Thor at his angriest. Nothing mattered beyond the excitement of this living, perpetual cascade of shining water. He was but a bug, an inconsequential flea against this monumental backdrop. All of heaven's passion came crashing down with the water here, and all of

Hades' angst. And he, a mere by-product of nature's wily pattern, not even fit to be humbled by its majesty.

He studied the deep, leafy foliage that enveloped the waterfall at its top and sides like a luxuriant, velvet, theatre curtain. Here the performance never ceased, there was no climax to thrill an audience, and the actors never took their final bow. That great curtain would not be drawn across the stage. The waterfall was its own endless encore, and the deafening roar from its pit more heart-stopping than any orchestra comprised of wind, string and brass.

It had taken him four days on foot to reach this spot deep in the heart of Venezuela's primary jungle. But here, he knew, pounded the true heartbeat he sought.

It was possible nobody had gazed on this sight before, or if they had, they would have walked away completely changed, unrecognizable. He had come to the jungle looking for temple ruins and had found instead an epiphany. There was no turning back. His mind reeled with the ecstasy of his discovery and at once everything he had ever known or seen or done was rendered totally insignificant. He had been born, if he had been born for any coherent reason whatsoever, for this moment.

He gazed blissfully, literally entranced, at the tumbling sheet of water and saw beyond its sparkling cloak Pacha Mama herself, the ancient Inca spirit of the earth, waiting to welcome him in her cool, smiling embrace.

Wordlessly he removed the pack from his back and placed it carefully on the rock on which he stood. He took off his hat and grey, soiled, travelling clothes and piled them together on top. Totally naked, he stepped into the swirling whirlpool and swam with broad, strong strokes towards the awesome shimmering sheet of plummeting water.

The following year the search party funded by National Geographic found his belongings and the strange one-word message scribbled on a notepad in his bag.

The guide scratched his head as he and his companions considered what possible reason he could have had for vanishing naked from this desolate spot.

“Something obviously disturbed his mind,” he said. “But why was he here? No temple ruins for miles around.”

One Venezuelan member of the search party peered over the edge of the empty, seemingly bottomless ravine beside them.

“Must have been a waterfall here aeons ago,” he speculated. “Tumbling down from that ridge there. But nothing but rainwater has kissed those cliffs for at least a million years.”

Don't Text Back

It was the weirdest thing. I woke up in the early hours, 3.16am, a cool, early spring morning in my £60-a-week provincial slumlet. That cute little 'text message' melody was dancing like a naughty elf not nine inches from my unsuspecting, sweet, slumbering ear.

"Jesus! For God's sake," I mumbled grouchily, always religious in my expletives.

Just a text, a-middle-of-the-flamin'-night, mega-intrusive text with a capital 'F'! What are friends for, eh? They're put on this goddamn earth to make sure a fellah can't get a decent night's sleep, that's what.

So I just lay there, desperate to return to my delectable dream involving the girl from the greasy spoon and free Full English on tap. I could just smell those sausages slipping seductively in their own fat. The girl was pretty mouth watering too.

But no way could I conjure it all up again. Once dreamed, it's dreamed. The girl probably went home with the trucker built like an entire rugby scrum, but not before he'd woofed down my Full English. I thought of those sizzling sausages slipping down some other fellah's throat. Not fair, life.

So there I am, tongue licking over my ungreased lips, tasting not spicy chipolatas but the lingering residue of last night's final fag.

I try to set the scenario up again. I am walking into the corner cafe, the girl behind the counter all in white and looking like a cross between a nurse and an angel. But this time she didn't look up, *wouldn't* look up. The only one who paid me any mind was the trucker at the corner table. *God, has he been working out since just a few seconds ago?*

Then it happened. An unmistakeable picture appeared in my mind, a familiar black shape that blocked out the waitress's more interesting charms. It was my mobile phone. I was *imagining* my mobile phone.

Its flap was open and in clear view was the Inbox message page:

CAN'T SLEEP SO Y THE HELL SHLD U? 8U x

Kathy! My ex-girlfriend. We'd split up three weeks ago, an amicable, mutual decision. Discounting the frying pan that whistled within a whisker of my ear and dented her favourite Renoir print on the wall behind me.

Then with relief, I realized: this was simply a hallucination. I was making the text up in my mind as a kind of excuse for my broken dream and the heartbreak loss of my angel/nurse and Full English.

With my face almost buried in the pillow, the wry smile of illumination that crossed my somnambulistic yet strangely handsome features was probably pretty well hidden by pillowcase.

I fell instantly back into a deep, welcome sleep.

The next day I awoke with the dustmen. Not literally, of course. Don't fancy any of them. But I came to – sort of – to the banging, clattering, slamming noises that accompany every Friday morning.

I went through the ritual of celebrating my 7,334th day on this planet with my usual enthusiasm, hampered only slightly by the realization that I had pulled two different coloured socks onto my lily white feet. I lay back on the bed wondering whether to have my first cigarette mid-costuming.

I stared up at the ceiling and then rolled over decisively to take a Gauloise from the blue packet. Time to consider whether I prefer yellow or green, I thought, staring hazily through the wispy smoke at my mismatched plates of meat.

It was then I remembered my disturbed dream and the 'imagined' text message in the middle of the night. I had to check what the real message was.

I rolled over and flipped open the black mobile, selecting the waiting message in one well practised movement.

CAN'T SLEEP SO Y THE HELL SHLD U? 8U x

Precisely the same as I had 'dreamt' it.

You know that feeling you get when you realize your team hasn't actually made it through, that it's all over, all the hopes and flag waving and cheering, all gone to nothing?

Or your mates have arrived but the beer hasn't and the telly's on the blink and you're going to have to tell them it's Scrabble or watch the match at someone's else's pad?

Yeah, just like that. I turned ice cold. I flushed hot. I felt sick.

I knew, absolutely knew, that I hadn't physically read that message in the middle of the night. And, anyway, it wouldn't have shown up on the screen as a new message as it did.

Yet, I knew it word for word. I'd read it in my mind's eye, in my half asleep, dozy state – somehow.

I checked it again. I checked the time it was sent: 3.16am. I even checked to see if there was a similar, earlier message that had been repeated. There wasn't.

I smoked the rest of that cigarette, and another one, and another, staring up at a spider on the ceiling while one green foot and one yellow foot crossed and crossed again in baffled agitation.

Later that day I was at my desk in the travel agency, half listening to old bull-nose Norris prattle on about demographics and presentations and targets and all that stuff, when my phone warbled again.

"Leave that!" Norris snapped. "Are you listening to me, Brewster?"

"Sir," I mumbled, acquiescent. It was just a part-time job while I waited for my last exam, but I needed the cash. So I made no move towards the phone in my pocket.

"If people didn't want to splash out on holidays they wouldn't come here in the first place, would they?" Norris was still on his high horse.

"No, Mr Norris." That was Jane, the sexy but dumb trainee from the council estate.

"Then make sure you persuade them to splash out Big Time! If they ask for Skegness suggest the Seychelles! If they want the day trip to Dieppe hand them a Caribbean cruise brochure. Titillate them. Believe me, they *want* to spend. They just need to be tempted..."

I was daydreaming, half asleep from my broken night. I'm in white shorts and t-shirt, sipping the most ridiculous looking drink you've ever seen – one that looks more like a Knickerbocker Glory. I'm peering over the deck rail of the Ocean Princess.

Small palm fringed islands shimmer in the distant haze, and beside me the long legged girl from the cafe (in a bikini!) picks at the overladen fruit in my drink with slender, pink nails.

As I dream, another image rudely interrupts my vision of paradise. The Hawaiian ukulele abruptly stops on C diminished.

Yet again, I could ‘see’ in my head the waiting message in my Inbox.

FANCY A BEER 2NITE? DOG AND DUCK 5.30. CLUB AFTER? NIGEL

I shook my head to clear my thoughts and reached in my pocket for my phone.

“Brewster! Put that down at once, if you please – I’m talking.”

I ignored him and fumbled with the buttons. Again I turned as ice cold as my fantasy Knickerbocker Glory as I read:

FANCY A BEER 2NITE? DOG AND DUCK 5.30. CLUB AFTER? NIGEL

Now it has to be said Nigel is a little predictable but even that didn’t stop me trembling as I got up and walked purposefully to the door. I couldn’t have predicted what the text was going to say. My brain was in a panic. I had to get away.

“Brewster! You walk out now, don’t bother coming back.” Norris was fuming.

“You need a break – book yourself a holiday,” I said, as I stepped out into the fresh air.

Some weeks later I was sitting my final exam in the main college hall, painfully aware that having lost my one and only source of income this test loomed even more important over my fragile future. No pressure, then.

Actually I was steaming on like... well, the Ocean Princess, and feeling pretty damned pleased with myself. I hadn’t mentioned this bizarre mobile phone business to anyone, not even to my best mate Nigel. I tried to put it safely on a backburner in order to clear my head for what was important in life – football, girls and (unfortunately) exams.

So I was sailing through, no sweat, until I got stuck on question xv111. My brain just stalled like my battered old 2CV.

“Jesus!” I said, but he refused to help. No inspiration came to me in a blinding flash of revelation.

I began to palpitate. I began to squirm. I looked at the fellows alongside me but all I could see were their arms enfolding their written gems like they were guarding the secrets of the Dead Sea Scrolls. Matthews looked up at me and grinned encouragingly.

I wished I could phone Nigel; he'd know. And if he didn't, he'd Google it. But phones of course are strictly banned from the examination hall. Even if you'd managed to smuggle one in, the beady-eyed examiner is well trained and eager to wheedle out the cheats.

Wait a moment, I thought to myself. If I can *receive* texts in my mind, maybe I can *send* them?

I summoned up the last of my intellectual energies (extremely limited at the best of times) and tried to 'picture' my mobile phone. It was lying in the bottom of my locker in a corridor outside along with 20 Gauloise and a £4 postal order from my gran. Don't laugh, it was very welcome, believe me.

I did it – I held a precarious image of my Samsung in my mind. Experimentally I began to mentally tap out a message to Nigel's number.

1. What are the chief exports of the South American continent?
2. Describe an Isthmus and explain how it is formed.
3. Give a short summary of how an Artesian Well functions.
4. Summarise the difficulties and manifest results of the merging of European and South American cultures and religions after the arrival of the Conquistadors.

God, this was taking an age! I nursed a hope that I had enough battery and inwardly smiled at the irony.

Ten minutes later I began to sweat again. The examiner would declare 'time up' any minute and I had completed everything except question xv111. My future burned before me, smouldering and in ruins.

The silence hung so heavy you could have used it as a doorstop. Suddenly I heard the distant but familiar warble of my mobile phone coming from the locker outside. It was very faint and hardly anyone else noticed it, but I had been waiting.

I closed my eyes and scrunched them tight. Then, slowly, I began to 'see' it – my incoming message box!

1. chief exports gold, silver, coffee, maize...

Give Nigel his due. He may be predictable but he doesn't muck about, and he doesn't ask awkward questions. It was all there, in full. Within minutes I put down my pen with a satisfied smile and folded my arms. I knew I had an A-star in the bag.

"Time's up, ladies and gentlemen," said the examiner, kindly.

Two weeks after that I got into another spot of bother, this time with the law. Unusual for me, as my admittedly unorthodox activities as anarchist, dissenter and apprentice antichrist are normally more subtle.

I blew a raspberry at a traffic warden I happened to see slapping a ticket on my dad's car, parked outside his office in town. To my astonishment the warden had had a bad day and came at me. Foolishly, I called him a word I wouldn't use in front of my gran and ran off, tossing the remains of a McDonald's milkshake (large, extra ice cream) over his nice new uniform.

After about five minutes crisscrossing this way and that across town, I collapsed panting into the bar at the *Dog and Duck.*

"Tom," called out a familiar voice. It was Nigel, but before I could reply, in marched that bloody traffic warden with a long, pink smudge on one arm and a flamin' policeman on the other.

"There he is, officer," yelled the warden. I hadn't reckoned on his tenacity or his fury. Must have been a brand new uniform.

I was marched off down to the station, the warden babbling on about young upstarts and wastrels and lack of respect etc etc. To paraphrase one of my dad's favourite jokes: *Take him downtown, Danno, and book him First Degree Milkshake.*

To my utter surprise, instead of laughing it off, the sergeant at the station rabbited on about Common Assault and GBH and ABH and told me I'd have to wait in a cell while various inquiries were made. Naturally they confiscated my cigarettes, lighter and phone.

Literally behind bars in the charge-room holding cell, I could hear the desk sergeant discussing the matter with the police officer and the warden. I couldn't believe they were making such a fuss.

So far I hadn't admitted a thing, and I could hear the warden being pressed about the need to be certain he had fingered the genuine culprit. They were working on the charge-sheet like there was no tomorrow.

This gave me an idea. I was by now well practised at 'conjuring' up my mobile phone in my mind and this I did, sending a text to Nigel:

URGENT TELL INTERESTED PARTIES WE HAD BEEN IN D&D FOR AN HOUR. DON'T TB

Then I rapped on my small barred window and demanded attention.

"If it's a question of an alibi, officer...?"

They all looked at each other in silence and then the desk sergeant unlocked the door to fetch me.

"Whatever happened to this poor gentleman in the execution of his fine work had nothing whatever to do with me," I began, theatrically rubbing my wrists as if they had just been released from heavy chains.

"It was him. It was. I know it was." The warden was too excitable. This was going to work in my favour.

"When you collared me I was enjoying a quiet drink with my pal Nigel Barrett during which we had been discussing such topics as the environment and soccer relegation for much of the morning. Check with him if you like. I'll give you his address and phone number."

I was released within minutes, the warden snarling at me as I walked defiantly from the station.

His arm was still smudged with greasy milkshake and I turned for a final word as I stepped through the door.

"Nice get-up. Pink goes well with the blue."

From then on things got even crazier.

Two nights later I woke up at 4am to that familiar 'text message' melody and, being quite used to the process by now, simply 'read it' in my mind.

I sat bolt upright and turned on the light.

U WRE RT! CAN'T LIVE W'OUT U. PILLS ONLY OPTION. GOODBYE X

I threw on my clothes and went hurtling over there as fast as I could in my clapped out, yellow 2CV.

I was hammering on the door like a lunatic and about to put my shoulder to it when I heard the sliding of bolts and it opened, revealing a sleepy-eyed Kathy in her night-dress.

"Are you OK?" I whispered urgently, putting my arms around her, coaxing the door shut with my foot and guiding her back to bed. "Lie there quietly while I call for an ambulance."

"Whatever for?" she whispered back, hoarse from broken sleep.

"You texted me. The pills!"

"What pills? What are you on about?"

She looked genuinely mystified and I stood there wondering what to make of it. Then I pulled my phone out and checked the last message. It wasn't there. What the hell? And what did 'You were Right' mean, anyway?

Inevitably I ended up sharing her bed for the rest of the night, which put my free-as-a-bird bachelor status back three months. She woke full of beans and singing her favourite Alicia Keys song while she made us breakfast and coffee.

I lay in her bed pulling deeply and thoughtfully on a Gauloise, bemoaning inwardly that now I'd *never* get rid of her. I didn't realize at the time how tragically wrong I was.

Later that week I bought a £6.75 box of chocolates and went to visit my gran in her nursing home.

"You look all in," she told me, as we settled down with a pot of tea by a French window looking out over the gardens. "You should be in here with me." Her bob of white hair bounced as she giggled girlishly at her own joke.

"I'm not getting enough sleep," I told her in utter truth.

"You should leave the girls alone," she admonished me gently. "How's that lovely Kathy? She's the one for you. I've always said it."

"She's fine, Gran. Actually we've split up."

I'd told her dozens of times but she preferred not to listen.

I stayed about an hour, talking about her childhood and mine, and just before I left she slipped something into my hand.

"I shouldn't encourage you, but go and buy yourself some of those smelly French cigarettes you like so much. It might calm you down and help you sleep."

"Thanks, Gran."

As I walked out of the nursing home I glanced at what I clutched in my sweaty palm before slipping it gracefully into my pocket. It was a shiny 50 pence piece.

"Thanks Gran," I smiled, genuinely grateful.

So I spent the rest of that summer receiving and sending texts through the medium of my own service provider cranium. I've seen the future, and although it may be shaped like an orange there's just a touch of dandruff. Just as strangely, I wasn't billed for any texts I sent 'mentally' and neither did they appear in my 'Sent' box. But the whole process was so exhausting and I felt so totally drained afterwards that I had to keep it to an absolute minimum.

Two months on I was again disturbed in the middle of the night by my phone's annoyingly jolly alert. I 'read it', as usual, in my mind:

CAN'T MAKE D&D 2NITE. DOG JUST DIED. NIGEL

Then I checked the actual phone. No message. Nothing. And neither had we arranged to meet up at the *Dog and Duck* as far as I remembered.

The next day I phoned Nigel ostensibly to tell him about my exam results. I had passed with flying colours.

"Thanks to you," I told him truthfully.

"Still don't know how you managed to smuggle your phone in without getting rumbled."

I never did enlighten him.

"Trade secret," I said mysteriously. "Thanks again for the other thing with the police, too."

"Sweet," he said. "All they did was phone me on my mobile to ask if I had spent any time with you that day. I told them we'd been supping pints for an hour and a half before they unceremoniously dragged you away to the dungeons."

"Enough to satisfy them they had an innocent man's blood on their hands. Incidentally, how's Jessie?"

"She's fine. She hasn't bitten anyone lately, if that's what you mean. Why are you asking? You *never* ask about my bloody dog."

"Just a bad dream. See you later."

"Congrats on your results. Celebration pint?"

"Maybe."

It was two weeks after that I got the two messages that turned my brain inside out.

First of all I was filling in behind the bar at the *Dog and Duck* when my message alert went off. I could hardly hear it above the din and didn't know exactly where I'd left the phone but 'pictured' it in my mind anyway.

CAN'T MAKE D&D 2NITE. DOG JUST DIED. NIGEL

Just like before. I threw down the cloth I had been using to wipe glasses and fumbled in a blind panic for my phone. This time it was a 'real' message.

I begged Fred for an early cut and raced over to see Nigel in the 2CV, windows flapping wildly in the wind.

"Run over by a lorry right outside," he told me. "Died instantly. Poor old Jess."

"She was a good dog. I know how upset your mum and dad must be, especially."

"Pop's only real friend," agreed Nigel, a tear threatening to spill from his lower lid.

The next day I battled through my sad little life as if I was in gumboots plodding through sticky mud nine inches thick. I just couldn't believe what was happening, far less explain it.

I lived in fear of my mobile phone. It sat there menacing on the bedside table like a sinister black portent, just waiting to herald the next round of bad news.

It came at dawn, after an utterly sleepless night.

I answered the alert for real, not wanting to go through the same sorry charade any more than I had to.

U WRE RT! CAN'T LIVE W'OUT U. PILLS ONLY OPTION. GOODBYE X

This time, unforgivably, I did nothing. My battered mind just didn't know whether it was coming or going. That's my excuse, and it's the only one I have left to cling to.

Three hours later the shocking loudness of the landline woke me up from a deeply entrenched, late morning sleep with its urgent, continuous ring.

It was Kathy's father. His sombre, measured tone told me he had some very bad news even before he said it.

There was an inquest of course and during the proceedings it came up that she had sent me – and others – a farewell text message.

It was easy to pretend my mobile phone had been in the other room and I hadn't read it until after her father called to tell me she had been found dead in bed from an overdose.

They asked me what she had meant by "You were right" but I just shrugged and said I had no idea. I couldn't tell them I had already received the very same message months before.

I have never talked about this to anyone until now. I knew exactly what Nigel would say and it wouldn't have helped: "I've heard of predictive texting but this is ridiculous."

After the funeral I used a hammer to crush my mobile phone to a pulp and buried it at the dump on the outskirts of town, miles away – way out of earshot.

I vow I'll never own one again, so if you still have my number, don't text back.

The Flag

The flag flicked his face in the black blistering mayhem, by turns caressing and then whipping his bloodied cheeks. The heavy stench of sulphur and cordite scorched the air, while overhead whizz-bangs and mortars beat his eardrums. But he did not flinch, he did not even blink as festoons of brightly coloured streams of fire shot off noisily in a dozen directions like some expensive firework display. More than once something flayed his upper body and legs, with a thud like a sledgehammer on a dozen pillows. Too painful to register any pain.

He kept his head down and only vaguely tasted blood as he tried to lick his desert-dry lips. The noise was deafening giving the scene an illusion of unreality. He had seen men fall to the right and left of him; worse, he had seen limbs flying absurdly through the air ahead of their surprised losers. Heads, even.

Comrades falling silently to the mud; they weren't even men, most of them. Boys. Boys who had gone gladly to the glory of it all, to the sound of drum and fife. Now only to eat the sodden, churned mud with their dying breath. A soft, unheeded choke as wide eyes sought, too late, answers they were too young to understand.

Their last living glance across the battlefield quagmire would have shown them his grey, meaningless flag. The flag they had so readily followed to hell, from mother's breast to the teat of grisly death. Hush. Goodnight and sweet dreams. May the sandman bring you rest.

He couldn't think coherently, but vague memories of home flickered so he could see in the mist a hint of Rosalind. She was there, by that crater full of torn, limbless bodies, beckoning. Or was she urging him back? No, she couldn't do that. There was no 'back' to return to, only forward, forward into the deafening melee.

Her arms hung listless at her side. There was nothing in her eyes but love. No hope, no plan, just helpless love. She floated above the carnage like an angel, untouched by the shells and shrapnel that spun like a maelstrom around her head.

He pressed on towards her, his boots sticking and sucking in the cloying mud where bits of humanity and abandoned weaponry churned like some sorcerer's soup from the apothecaries of Hades. One foot felt warmer than its partner and he looked down to find its leather boot had been all but ripped away. He stared bewildered at his bared toes, surprisingly as yet un-muddied in the brown jelly of death. He twiddled his big toe, as he did in the bath when he was ten. Absorbed. Meditative. He must keep this young toe safe: Perhaps unnoticed all the way down there, partly buried in the sludge, its useless ex-boot laying around it like a cracked eggshell.

He lifted his head as another whizz-bang smacked above, not twenty yards away. Yet he didn't even tremble. Was that gas he could smell? So many weeks of fear had left permanent traces of it in his nostrils; he couldn't tell anymore. Anyway he no longer had his gas mask. It seemed a pitiful thing to carry as you strode with whatever bravado you could muster into a solid wall of flak; you might just as well open an umbrella as you plunge into a bottomless chasm.

Rosalind was gone. But now he could see Jack, calling to him over the foxholes. No words came through the din but he knew what Jack was saying. So many happy times he had heard him call 'Daddy!' and he had thrilled to each and every one. Incredible that a word as ridiculously ubiquitous as 'taxi' or 'hotel' can yet be so utterly, undeniably personal. "Daddy," Jack soundlessly yelled, and he raised his arm to acknowledge his son's beseeching plea.

"Jack," he mouthed back, his lips tasting of blood and mud and unrecognizable fear. Jack! He pulled his denuded foot from the sucking, cloying mud, using the flag he was carrying as a walking stick and ploughed forward. Jack!

Again the flag whipped his face and for an instant stole his view. When again he could peer ahead through the thick mantle of black cloudbursts he could see only the barbed wire and littered bodies, thrown haphazardly in all sorts of bizarre shapes over ammo boxes and fallen helmets. Next to each body, a Lee-Enfield poked out of the mud like a grave marker, its bayonet glinting faintly in the murk.

Jack! Jack!

He stopped but not because of the familiar rattle of a sub-machine gun he had heard nearby. Ours? Theirs? It didn't really matter. Such mundane distinctions were no longer of concern to him. They were all instruments of death, whether aimed at him or aimed at his enemies. His only possible purpose was to clutch the flag, press on... to Jack.

He felt another thud like a punch in his upper torso and he knew he had been hit. He twisted but did not fall. There was no pain, or if there was he didn't recognise it as such. There was just the smell; the smell of cordite and rot, death and decay.

His eyes misted and he considered the possibility that his march had at last been marched. He summoned the last of his strength to pound the short flagpole into the soft mud at his feet, and leaned against it utterly wearied.

"Jack," he called out loud, but could barely hear himself. He forced his dying eyes open in a last attempt to pierce the gloom ahead.

He could see him. He was running towards him, his shorts and school blazer pristine and absurd on the battlefield, oblivious to all but his father.

He could feel him, he could feel his six-year-old arms wrapped around his failing legs. He must find the strength. He must be the pillar, the rock he had always been for his son. He clutched the flagpole tight. He could feel Jack's little fingers digging into the backs of his legs and his little wet face pressed deep against his waist.

"Daddy!"

He had carried his flag to the end.

At the sound of his mother's voice, the small boy instantly released his bear-hug hold from the soldier's stone cold legs.

"Sebastian, get down from there." His mother's command rang stern and clear above the happy din of other children playing nearby in the sunlit park garden. "Come off that statue at once."

Obediently Sebastian clambered from the plinth, clutching for a moment the soldier's bared foot in its ripped leather boot to help keep his balance.

He looked back once as he jumped lightly to the ground. He admired the stern-faced, resolute figure hugging his solid flag as if it were real, as if it were truly blowing in the winds of battle.

Sebastian wanted to be a soldier when he grew up. Just like him.

Des Res in SW7

I am – was – an estate agent. The lowest of the low to some people, ranked somewhere between traffic wardens, tax inspectors and newspaper reporters. A man not to trust. Whatever I said had to be wrong. It was presumed to be in my nature. A profession born of lies and half-truths. It wasn't really the way it was, but it was certainly the public perception. That's all behind me now. These days I just sit here at this little table by the window remembering, week in, month out. Sometimes on bad days they bring me extra medicine, which I try every trick in the book not to take. They're shrewd though, these carers. I don't often get away with it and down it goes. Then I spend the rest of the afternoon feeling drowsy and a little on the giddy side.

All for the best, I suppose.

44, Cornwall Gardens was an estate agent's dream. Its very location meant it would sell itself. Slap bang in the middle of one of the most coveted areas of central London: the white pillared Eden of South Kensington, SW7. Never in my 20-year career at James, Carstairs and Brown had such a sales opportunity presented itself. All three flat owners at that address decided to sell up at the same time. And, of course, they all came to us as the premier estate agent of the higher echelons.

A stone's throw from Hyde Park and the best museums, the square had its own private 'residents only' garden in the middle (everyone got a golden key) and bijou mews cottages at the western end set the final seal on its desirability.

Go there now and you'll have a bit of a shock. They all think I'm mad but they are just covering up the unpalatable truth. Nobody can understand what happened so they just ignore it, pretend everything is perfectly normal. Anyone like me who still screams in the night, they lock up. No golden key for me.

Go on, I defy you. I dare you. Get along there, it's easy – Gloucester Road tube is just around the corner. Piccadilly Line. You'll see straight away that something's... wrong. But a word of warning: Don't go at night.

I went at night. Well, early evening actually. It looked absolutely wonderful then – heaven. I stood on Otto von Blick's balcony looking down over the park and breathed in the freshness that is SW7. I could hear the birds singing in the trees and turned to tell von Blick.

"Just listen to those…" I stopped mid sentence. The expression on his face was horrible, like a man facing Inquisition thumbscrews in some dark, deep dungeon.

"What the devil is wrong?" I asked, hastily putting down my orange juice and hurrying to his side. "Are you ill?"

He told me a story then that every instinct rejects as utter nonsense. No ghosts – nothing going bump in the night. But a chilling story of the pure supernatural nonetheless.

I struggled only a little with his accent.

"I stood on the balcony, just like you now. It was a wonderful evening and the birds were singing then too. A sense of perfect peace came upon me. Perfect peace."

He stopped and it seemed as if that was it, nothing more to tell.

"Go on," I encouraged.

"Perfect peace. Hardly hear any traffic at all, even though the busy Cromwell Road is only yards away. Then it hit me – I really couldn't hear any traffic. No traffic at all. It was uncanny. Here I stood in the middle of one of the busiest cities in the world and it was just as if I was in the middle of the Black Forest."

"Sounds perfect," I ventured.

"Perfect?" he scoffed. " Yes, you would think that. So did I – at first. But then I started straining my ears to hear anything familiar in a city; a car horn, a passing jet heading in or out of Heathrow, even voices. But – nothing. Nothing."

"You're just trying to hike up the price," I joked, but it failed to lighten the mood. Instead, he clammed up.

Otto von Blick wasn't about to shake himself out of it so I decided to abandon the conversation for that night. We shook hands and I promised to telephone to make another appointment to discuss details but it was like talking to a zombie. His eyes didn't see me any more than his ears could hear me.

The next day was no better. I phoned very early in the evening to catch him before he had a chance to hit the bottle.

"Herr von Blick?" I began.

" It was worse last night, after you left. I stared out over the park from the balcony and at first it was just like before. Peaceful. Birdsong. Rustling leaves."

"Were you having a nightcap before turning in?" He ignored the implication.

"Everything turned dark around the edges. The scene... deepened, somehow. It no longer seemed like a country idyll. It was a jungle."

"Perhaps the gardeners have been a little lax?" Again he ignored me.

"...I could hear screeching parrots, chattering monkeys – nothing but jungle sounds – louder and louder and louder until I had to cover my ears. I ran back inside to get away from it. But when I looked out I could just see the dark, silhouette of deep primary jungle. No street lamps, no headlights, no windows opposite. Nothing but the sights and sounds of jungle. I'll go mad if I don't get out of here. You must sell it – YOU MUST SELL IT!"

"Calm down, please. That's what we're here for. Perhaps we could arrange another meeting? There are a few details still to iron out. Paperwork. You understand."

The phone went dead and I was left there feeling stupid, listening to the dialling tone. I should have called him straight back, that was the professional thing to do. But, frankly, I was a little spooked by this crazy customer. In any event, I decided to call him the next day.

I wish I'd called immediately, laid this thing, whatever it was, to rest. But I didn't and now I'm sitting here in this God forsaken hospital because I'm the only one who realizes what happened.

Go on, go there. See for yourself. You think I'm mad like I thought *he* was mad. But you go, see what you make of it. Stand outside 44 Cornwall Gardens and take a good look. It's a square of about 200 houses in the main part. Beautiful they are. All white Georgian pillars and giant arched balcony windows.

You'll see something strange. Something people don't talk about. Tell me what you think. You'll join me in here soon enough. Mark my words. Des Res, sure enough. But there's something inexplicable. You'll mark it. I'd take you myself only it's time for my medicine, and they wouldn't let me go anyway.

All the houses are double fronted, see, two pairs of gleaming white pillars side by side, all around the square. Except... except when you get to Number 42. There's only one pair of pillars outside Number 42. Why? WHY? Why indeed?

Oh look. See nurse hurrying over to her agitated patient sitting at his solitary table by the window. I'm here! *Private, secluded situation: Ideal for hermit or monk.*

"Don't get excited now. Take some of this... easy now."

I know I look old and forlorn, as attractive as a slum terrace with a yellow wheelie bin jammed in a tiny front garden. *A cosy, well lived-in property, would suit first time buyer, preferably psychiatric DIY enthusiast.*

I imagine being her, my nurse, watching my crumpled face pull a disgusted look as my tongue seeks to wipe all trace of the tranquillising medicine from my lips. *Much sought after location, close to all amenities, school, supermarket and straightjacket.*

They don't tell you why, do they? But I know. I know.

Yes, I'm calmer now, but see the fear still lurking in my eyes. *A loon with a view.*

I went back. The next day I went back. I couldn't believe the change in von Blick. After just 48 hours he looked completely different. A wasted soul with haunted, drained eyes. He opened the door an inch and refused to let me enter. I could see he was utterly crazed. Like me now, I suppose.

"May I come in?" I said, as gently as I could.

He stared back at me with those empty eyes.

"Just sell it. Get me out of here. Go away."

He closed the door and no amount of ringing the doorbell would bring him out. I turned and went back to the office. I was confused and didn't know what to do. I thought about asking Hetherington about Number 44 Cornwall Gardens but decided against it. He would take a pragmatic line. An estate agent had no business getting spooked. Get in there and sort it out, would be his advice. Tie up the sale and go home and kick the cat. Or the wife.

I did go home but the whole thing preyed on my mind so much I couldn't go to bed before I'd tried von Blick on the phone once more. It rang five times and when he answered he seemed to know at once it was me.

"*Listen!*"

I did my best but I could hear nothing.

"The sea. Can you hear the sea?"

"I'm afraid I... wait a minute... yes, I can hear waves, crashing against the shore."

"Pounding. The waves are pounding. Seagulls."

It was true. I could hear it quite clearly over the telephone. Then I supposed I might be listening to his TV.

"Is this a game, Herr von Blick?"

But there was something about the rushing of the waves. The unmistakeable sucking noise as they pulled back from the beach stopped me short. Somehow I knew this was real.

"The pounding of the waves. There's a storm coming."

It all grew so loud I could hardly hear him.

"Herr von Blick? Are you alright?"

Then came the most monstrous, blood curdling scream I have ever heard in my life. I slammed down the phone and ran out of my apartment as fast as I could, ignoring the startled pleas of my wife standing in the bedroom doorway in her nightie.

I was trembling as I struggled to open the door of my Seat and pulled away from the kerb with a lurch. It took me just ten minutes to drive down from Notting Hill Gate but when I pulled up outside Number 44 Cornwall Gardens it was... gone!

Like the madman I have perhaps since become I tore at my hair as I stood outside on the pavement, turning first this way and then that.

"Herr von Blick!" I screamed. "Herr von Blick!"

When the police came I was already the broken man you see today. I was staring at the house numbers – there could be no mistake. There was Number 42 and to one side was Number 40. But to the other... Number 46. One set of white stucco pillars stood before me – the only single set in the entire square. Check it out for yourself. Number 44 had vanished. Oh there's no gap there – the join is seamless, but it's gone all the same.

They restrained me after the neighbours complained that I had screeched up in my little black car, screaming at the top of my voice. It was 11pm after all.

They took me away and eventually I was brought here. But I know what they've done. They can't fool me. They've changed all the numbers in Cornwall Gardens as if nothing had happened.

Number 46 has now become Number 44, and so on all the way around. No questions asked, because everyone is afraid to ask questions.

But I know. That's why I'm here. *I know*. You go and take a look. You'll see that I'm right.

Why take my word for it? I'm just an estate agent.

The Pope's Testicles

For a long time I stared at the panelled walnut front door with its ugly gargoyle knocker and knew exactly how a burglar or a Jehovah's Witness must feel lurking on some stranger's doorstep. Cautiously, I turned the key in the lock and allowed myself a satisfied smirk at the comforting *click*. At least she hadn't changed the locks. My smile was more like a huge sigh made flesh with a standing ovation of teeth.

The door pushed open easily, chaffing a little on the rough bristle Home-Sweet-Home mat with a sound like surf over a pebble beach. I didn't want to play my hand too early, before I'd had a chance to assess the enemy's strength. I ventured an exploratory soft cough followed by a small "hello?"

No answer. And no sound of movement anywhere in the house either. Oh God, I thought, she's sulking down the shops or at her sister's.

It hadn't been the worst of rows, in my opinion. I mean it wasn't flying teacups or four-letter curses spat with epileptic stammer and spittle. I would call that one Rage Red. But Josie's not like that. She's more of a Moribund Mauve. Perhaps this was a degree a two darker than usual, I conceded.

It was the subject that was so sensitive. I learned long ago to steer well away from any mention of children. Having them, I mean. Ever since 'The Tests' it was a topic more taboo than the Pope's testicles. Frankly, I wasn't all that bothered – which I suppose made it so much worse in her eyes. I could think of gloomier fates than a life without noisy, runny-nosed little tykes running all over the house screaming 'I want – I want!'

But she *needed* them, see. Oh, she *needed* them so much. Personally I wondered what all the fuss was about. I mean, I don't think I would have actually sought out a partner who couldn't have kids, but having got one I couldn't see that it was all that bad. Nice quiet existence.

So I suppose that while I just sort of casually shrugged it all off, she was secretly in turmoil. She hid it well, though. Until the day my mother dropped that awful clanger and Josie just exploded like the suppressed steam engine she was.

We were showing Mum over the newly decorated house and we reached the guest room, which is just a standard box room. I should explain that she's sweet and means well but she's getting on a bit and can sound, frankly, a bit *distracted* at times. OK, *potty* is probably more accurate.

"Aaah, blue!" she exclaimed pleasantly. "Wouldn't this have been simply perfect for a nursery?"

Well of course Josie burst into tears and Mum didn't know where to put her face and in the end I decided it was better just to take her home and look after Josie later. Mum wasn't helping, see. She simply didn't understand the damage she had caused.

So now I was back and preparing to face the music. But I could hear absolutely nothing – not even a soft symphony.

"Hello?" I called again, as I peeked into the lounge. There was no reply and at first I saw just an empty room. I was about to check the kitchen when I saw her – curled up in a big armchair and still sobbing silently. I could have sworn I had already looked in that chair.

"Mum's really sorry," I whimpered, doing my best to pour proverbial oil on troubled waters.

"I want to talk about our unborn babies," she said quietly, her words chilling and stark.

It was quite the most astonishing thing I had ever heard her say.

I cannot describe how passionately we hid from this subject, with a determination that protected us both. It was simply a topic never to be taken from the closet, dusted off and aired for debate. And now this 'stranger' sitting on the armchair, legs tucked under her, announced she wanted to talk about it as she might the price of cheese or the latest weather bulletin.

It was akin to turning on the TV news to see the Pope dropping his trousers or lifting his skirts or whatever it is the Pope would do.

After years of fruitless IVF and hormone treatment Josie had emerged broken, exhausted and devoid of any hope. She had surrendered to the inevitable with a despair that was heartbreaking. The only alternative – adoption – was out of the question because she was certain she could never bond with someone else's baby, however maternally she tried to clasp it to her bosom.

The tear-stained handkerchief she clutched tight against her face told me these waters were going to need a lot more oil than your economy-sized three-in-one.

It wasn't like Josie at all but the angry words raged on unchecked. She was getting it all off her chest – but as she got more and more personal about my poor old Mum I found myself defending her despite that insensitive gaffe.

"Oh, come on Josie," I whined. "She didn't mean anything by it. She's 80 for heaven's sake. Diplomacy's the first in the lifeboat when ships start to rot."

She looked at me as if I'd just raised the flag for apartheid, daytime TV, or non-organic eggs or something. It was pure Rage Red. I prepared to duck the teacups. Whatever happened to Moribund Mauve or even Prickly Pink?

"She's always hated me for not giving her grandchildren," she blurted, through tommy-gun sobs. "She goes on and on about that Maureen. *Bet she's married with ten kids by now…*" She was trying to mimic my Mum's Yorkshire accent, which got my goat a bit.

"Four," I said, stupidly. Maureen was an ex-girlfriend.

"*What!!?*"

"Maureen. She's got a family of four."

"Oh *really*? And how do you know that? Are you the lucky father?"

"Mum still sees her from time to time, when she goes over to Claygate cemetery to see Dad's grave. Maureen lives over that way."

Graves were a spookily appropriate focus right about now. I was digging myself a hole big enough for the entire Borgia dynasty.

But Josie just totally buckled, mentally and physically. I took her in my arms to support her as she wailed, "I always wanted us to have a family, a warm, loving family. Never dreamed life would be so barren."

I mumbled some placatory platitudes but she was plummeting over the edge.

"…I love *you*, Josie – I wasn't attracted to you because I thought you were some sort of over-ripe fertility machine. You made me happy, that's why I had to marry you."

"*Made* you happy?"

"*Make* me happy. You make me happy."

"You said 'made'. Past tense." Petulant, she broke away from my arms and turned her face from mine. It was a Cold War and fast downgrading far beyond Moribund Mauve.

"No. You *make* me happy. You always did, always will."

"Don't tell me you don't watch that Maureen in the supermarket! With her dozens of kids and you, with your tongue hanging out, wishing you were pushing that trolley stuffed to burst with nappies and rusks and talcum powder." She said it to the wall as if I wasn't worth addressing directly.

She'd never been like this, not once in ten years together. I'd seen her angry but never so utterly distressed. She would never show herself to be so vulnerable. It just wasn't in her nature. I thought a little joke might help.

"Makes me sneeze… talc," I said quietly. I felt her wet, reddened eyes boring into mine as I tried vainly to regain her trust.

She was silent for a full minute and finally took my hand and raised it to her lips to kiss. But it was a sad kiss, not a kiss of adoration. Like a last fond farewell.

"Talc makes you sneeze," she repeated quietly. It wasn't a question, but I answered as if I thought it was.

"I come out in hives."

For the first time that evening, she smiled, but it was a strange, enigmatic smile. I suddenly felt as if I didn't know her at all, whereas I stood exposed and transparent as a shop window. The torrent of sorrow had finally stopped flowing from her green eyes, and now I felt like a small boy under the wisdom of her gaze.

She dropped my hand and walked serenely to the living room door where she turned and glanced back at me, saying nothing. Then she disappeared into the hall, presumably to go to the bathroom to fix herself up.

I poured myself a stiff whisky. It had been a harrowing evening and I was still worried about my mother. She'd been bundled off home like a naughty child.

I replaced the stopper in the decanter and then changed my mind, taking it out again to pour Josie a glass too. She didn't generally take whisky but we needed all the help we could get tonight.

I tipped back my head and threw my first straight down my throat. It felt better already. Then I heard the soft *ping* from my laptop, heralding incoming mail.

I poured another Scotch and put the glass down carefully by the side of my black Toshiba as I activated the cursor.

I smiled with relief as I read the words on the screen. "I LOVE YOU, BUG-HEAD." Only a girl-child like Josie would send an email from another room just yards away. But the hairs on the back of my neck prickled as I noticed something that made the stem glass in my hand tremble.

There, in total repose on the other side of the table – serene and sinister – lay Josie's *untended* laptop and I-phone. Mystified I put down the glass and rushed upstairs calling her name.

"Josie! Josie!"

I threw open door after door but she had simply vanished. Large as life just moments before, but now she was gone. I was alone in an empty house.

There was one door still unchecked. The boxroom. Slowly I turned the handle and peeked inside. My burning brow turned damp with instant beads of perspiration.

There in the gloomy interior I could just make out two small cots against opposite walls. Above each, paper mobiles of animal shapes moved lazily, almost imperceptibly, in the draught caused by the open door. A musical box tinnily played Brahm's Lullaby. Baffled and fascinated I stepped carefully into the room, better to see two tiny faces asleep on two tiny pillows. The walls my mother had so tactlessly described as reminiscent of a nursery were no longer blue but alive with scenes from fairy tales; happy children scampered up hill and down dale, red-capped elves sat with their hands wrapped around their knees atop toadstools and cosy gingerbread cottages beckoned from a hillside.

As I gazed wide-eyed, and advanced cautiously on the cots, a soft voice urged, "*hush* – they're asleep!" It was Josie's voice. I whirled around expecting to see her standing there with a finger against her lips but… there was no-one. I gasped and turned back to the room to yet another shock. The blue walls were back and the cots gone. The small guest bed stood in the centre of the room as it was before.

I tore downstairs to double-check the email and didn't know if I was relieved or certifiable to see it still there, bold as brass: *I LOVE YOU, BUG-HEAD.*

The urgent ring of the telephone added to the cacophony in my bewildered brain.

It was my smug sister-in-law, calling from her smug semi three miles away on the smug side of town.

"It's Josie," she said simply.

"What is?" I answered. I was confused, my mind whipping in circles.

"I'm very worried."

"Me too." I started. "I…"

But, as usual, this lady wasn't for interrupting. "She's in some kind of fit. It's been hours. High fever, mumbling all sorts of nonsense about talcum powder and sneezing."

"Hours?" I said incredulous, glancing across at the untouched whisky I had poured for her, lonely and waiting on the drinks cabinet. "Impossible – she was right here, a moment ago."

She ignored me, a thing she was fond of doing.

"She grabbed a taxi straight over when you took your mum home after your blazing row…"

"Row?" I blurted angrily. "There was no row. She was upset, that was all."

"Well, she said there had been some kind of tiff, she wasn't specific. She keeps it all inside, does Josie. What happened?"

I just couldn't think straight for a moment.

"Nothing, really. I think there was something she wanted to get off her chest but didn't know how. I'll be right over."

Her voice brightened. "Well, whatever it was she's forgiven you. The last thing she said was 'I love you, bug-head.' That's when I decided I should call."

"Yeah, thanks – I'll be ten minutes. Tell her I wouldn't change anything for the world."

Wreck

Honolulu never really lets you go. However hard you try to leave, you find yourself cast back on its shores like the leis that the garlanded hula girls toss onto the soft caressing waves for the delight of tourists.

To the casual observer, Barney Wilson's gaze back towards the Waikiki beach lagoon and the far off Diamond Head volcano was studied nonchalance, but Barney was not as calm as he seemed. He stood in the cockpit of the 30 foot motor launch Buccaneer and, with one practised hand on the wheel, paid as much attention to where he'd been as to where he was going.

Diamond Head – climb that peak to its upper lip, and you find yourself in a bizarre crater-plateau, millions of years old. Green and lush now – but once, in a dim and distant past when dinosaurs ruled the earth, no place to play ball. Not unless you wanted to fry in molten lava at several thousand degrees centigrade.

Barney looked over at his pal Ben 'Nevis' McCleod who was surveying the diving equipment as the Buccaneer sliced effortlessly through the white tipped waves and out towards the open sea. Nevis was a short, stocky Scot with a wit and tongue as barbed as his harpoon gun. At 50, he was fifteen years older than Barney and at times the extra experience showed. Barney smiled now as he listened to the Glaswegian expletives which flowed as Nevis checked valves, face masks and bottles of compressed air. It had all started as a drunken idea in the Beachcomber piano bar. Wouldn't it be a blast, Barney had suggested, if they took a few days off from the diving school they ran along the beach from Waikiki, and did a tour of the islands? Heaven knows, they worked hard enough. Teaching rich kids how to scuba and buddy-breathe, how not to get the bends, and how, generally, to jump into deep water without getting into *hot* water.

Barney, like Nevis, loved Hawaii. He had first come to the islands in '81 with a Trade Delegation and – just like those leis that always come floating back, found he just couldn't stay away from the golden, sandy shores. He was a public relations man. It was a job he had once heard described as 'putting up the signs before the circus comes to town'. But in truth he didn't much care for the circus, and he certainly didn't like putting up the signs.

So he quit his job. His next act was throwing away the suit and tie he was forced to wear along with a fixed smile practically every minute of his working day.

The smile stayed though, and became even wider, inspired by genuine contentment. He found a cheap place on Atkinson Drive in the middle of town, surrounded by the tall palms and cool waterways that make Honolulu so attractive, and started a new life as, he now had to admit, a beach bum. A strange career change for a 35-year-old bachelor with a British university background and a degree in just about everything but anything he was remotely interested in.

It wasn't long before he met Nevis – nicknamed, naturally, after the mountain. That they should meet was almost inevitable, like dregs settling in the bottom of a barrel – in their case most likely a beer barrel. Barney and Nevis washed up on the all-embracing Hawaiian shores along with other pieces of human flotsam; war-maimed casualties of love and life, nursing their respective wounds with plentiful doses of self prescribed medicine with names like Jim Beam, Lambs Navy, or good old Teachers.

Nev was a diver and had been trying – singularly unsuccessfully – to start a diving school at Waikiki. The local kids proved to be rather too absorbed in the almost obligatory Hawaiian sport of surfing and a twilight world of illicit drugs deals conducted on the beaches at dusk among the notorious pimps and hash dealers.

They teamed up and the marriage of convenience proved to be a happy one. Following Barney's advice, Nevis turned his attention to the tourist market and they aimed their services directly at the big hotels on and around the magnificent beaches. It worked like a dream. Nev taught Barney how to sink like a stone with 25lb of scuba gear on his back, and Barney taught him how to stay afloat in the deep, treacherous seas of business. They soon became known as *Barney and Ben the Underwater Men.*

Now, between them, if not exactly rich, they had at least paid for a des-res beachhouse which was big enough for them to share without living in each other's pockets too much. The bar was always well stocked.

“What time do ye think we’ll get there?” Nev’s deep baritone voice boomed across the soft sounds of the Pacific Ocean, which today lived up to its name and reputation as the ‘peaceful’ giant, and the planet’s largest body of water.

Barney looked at his Omega Seamaster’s Professional diver’s watch, an almost supernaturally precognitive gift from his former fiancé shortly before their acrimonious split three years earlier. He remembered her words as he courteously expressed shock at the expense of such a fine gift. “There’s no time like the present,” she had quipped. “And no present like the time.”

Unfortunately present time now ticked on separately for both of them, and in opposing hemispheres, but the expensive watch had proven a godsend in his new chance career as a diver.

“Guaranteed to work at 2,000 feet,” an impressed Nevis had told Barney soon after they met. “But at that depth you’d be dead; fish feed. The only time that would concern you would be from eternity-oclock to five-past-forever.

“You wouldn’t need a two thousand pound watch for that.”

“We should make Kauai by around four, bang on schedule,” Barney informed Nev now, as he steered the Buccaneer slightly to starboard to meet the wash of a passing cruise ship.

The plan was to take in all the main islands in one round trip, leisurely stopping at the main resorts at the end of each day. Allowing for frequent pleasure dives, which they did more to keep their hand in than anything else, the whole adventure was scheduled to last just over a week.

Nevis knew of some pretty un-missable drinking holes in Nihue and Kahoolawe, where the company would be equally ‘interesting’, so – if it came to any sort of itinerary – that was it.

Kauai was their first stop, one easy day north west from Oahu. Barney returned a friendly wave to some revellers on a beautiful square-sailed lugger, heading the other way towards Oahu. These were busy waters in the tourist season – which was pretty much all the year round in this heaven of steady and very comfortable climate.

Barney smiled as he watched Nevis work, singing some Highland-inspired song from Brigadoon about a girl with heather in her heart and a Hollywood actor on her arm. Strange that all the Scotsmen he had ever met, thought Barney, sang deeply heartfelt, passionate songs of regret about a country they rarely seemed inclined to return to. Every bar in the world had such a Scot.

Barney continued to smile into the sea breeze as he realized both men were happy. They restricted their romantic associations for the most part to 'visiting' tourist girls – no involvement, no kickback. They were part of the romantic time these girls would find on the magical islands, and, when it was over – it was over. A goodbye kiss on the beach (they NEVER went to the airport to see them off) and it was back to normality and *freedom.* Neither man wanted to be tied down again by women. Nev had been married once for twenty years. It had all ended in tears.

Barney's girl, Felicity, had been a high roller. The daughter of a High Court judge and an artist (whose fame had made her a household name, at least in some households, mainly in places like Chelsea, Cheltenham and Chiddingfold.)

Felicity was used to having everything, and chief amongst them was her own way. It took three short years for them to realize their differences. Barney was in the gutter, peering up at the stars. Felicity was already up there, gazing down and offering something of a royal wave and a leg-up. It wasn't going to work.

No, Barney and Nevis had now found their niche – laughing losers in an endless sea of non-commitment and freedom. *Banking off a north east wind, sailing on a summer breeze, skipping over the ocean like a stone.* The words of the old song sang in his head as Barney opened the throttle and purred the motor cruiser out into the open water.

The next three days put them a little behind schedule, thanks to a head-thumping 'morning after' in the Oyster Bar on staggeringly beautiful Nihue. They woke up in a room above the bar, Barney sprawled fully dressed across his bed, Nev still on the floor, one arm stretched optimistically across the valance of his own bed.

A broken and un-smoked cigarette was balanced precariously between his fingers. He laboured himself into a sitting position on the edge of the bed, snapped the cigarette properly in two and lit up the stub.

"Good morning, chum,' slurred Nev, striving with great pains to open one eye and observe his friend the other side of the room. "Great night."

“Was it?” said Barney, rubbing his throbbing head with both hands. “Can’t remember.”

Within an hour they were whipping south easterly across the open ocean just three miles off the coast from Honolulu where they had started. Their adventure took them on an elliptical course requiring a ‘u-turn’ after visiting the outer islands of Kauai and Nihue.

“Don’t know about yous but I could do wi’ a dip,” intoned Nevis in his broad, heavy accent. “Don’t think the wee barmaid put enough *watter* in me malt.”

“We’re behind schedule – but who gives a damn?” grinned Barney, and they dropped anchor for a couple of hours leisurely diving.

The depth sounder put them in 20 feet of water although the charts were a little unclear about that. “We may be on a reef, mebbe,” observed Nev, the more experienced boatman.

Together they prepared their equipment and Nev ran all the last minute checks, as he always did. Finally he loaded the spear-guns and handed one to Barney.

“Ye never know yer luck,” he grinned. “We may get a tuna for the pot or a barracuda to sell in the markets.”

As always, Nev was first to drop backwards over the side of the boat, and surfaced to watch as Barney did the same. Then came that moment of exhilaration that Barney could never quite get used to – a kick of the flippers to start the descent into the warm, clear water.

As they dived, Barney smiled behind his mask as he remembered Nev telling him, “One thing about divers – they hate getting wet! Cold and wet – divers can’t stand it.”

Immersed though they were, it was true there was no hint of cloying wetness against the skin. Every part of the body felt dry and warm, apart from the hands, left un-gloved for dexterity.

Barney watched the bubbles from Nev’s mask as the second man indicated the steep, sandy incline off to their left. Nev had been right – they were above a reef which gave way to a sudden drop to the ocean’s true depth.

Nev was stabbing his right hand downward to suggest they should explore deeper where there was more likelihood of some interesting sport. Unlike in British waters, the use of spear-guns by scuba divers was illegal here – but, hell, there didn't seem to be too many patrol cars around, thought Barney.

Barney was busy listening to his own hollow, echoing breath and feeling the strange sensations of growing depth pressure when he suddenly became aware of Nev's excitement.

He seemed to have spotted something, perhaps 50 feet below them, but what? Barney could see nothing, the distance distorting every detail despite the clear, calm water. He could make out colour – and shoals of beautiful darting fish. But nothing else.

He kicked out his flippers to follow Nev's effortless merman descent. Then, suddenly, he saw it – the unmistakeable outline of a wreck.

It was, even to his untutored eye, an ancient vessel, perhaps a seventeenth or eighteenth century man-o-war. One of three masts was still tall enough to be worthy of the name, and much of the wooden hull and infrastructure was instantly recognisable despite centuries of algae and barnacle encrustation. Schools of vividly hued fish darted first this way and then that above what remained of the decking.

But, strangest of all, there was a bizarre shape crowning the centre of what had to be the sunken ship's main deck. A small boat shape, undoubtedly, but – and here Barney wanted to pinch himself to make sure he wasn't dreaming – *modern!*

The two divers explored the wreck in perfect conditions, the ocean flattering their limb movements so they looked both graceful and expressive like underwater ballerinas. Twice, to Barney's dismay, Nev ducked under some rotting, fallen timber to explore deeper inside the vessel. Then, horrified, Barney saw his friend clearly signal a reassuring 'thumbs up' before disappearing into the wreck itself, his speargun thrust out before him.

A sunken wreck was always an attractive playground for confident swimmers – such as conger eels and shark.

Barney said later that it was the most nerve-racking two minutes of his life but eventually Nev reappeared with an unidentifiable object under his left arm. It was long and thin, but its identity was disguised under a thick crust of limpet-like sealife.

Nevis signalled towards the surface with a nod of his head and handed Barney his speargun before both men headed up towards the sunlight, eager but not too fast.

Back on board the Buccaneer they whipped off their masks and headgear to survey their find. It was an extraordinarily decorative telescope, and just a few minutes careful sponging was enough to reveal its true, indescribable beauty.

Barney whistled through his teeth. "That looks like gold to me," he said.

"That it is, me lad," said Nevis. "Without a shadow of a doubt. And there's plenty more treasure down there, too, I can tell you that."

"Got to be worth a fortune," replied Barney. "God, we're rich! We've hit the mother lode this time."

But both men knew there were rules about this sort of thing, and rules mean complications. Taking the telescope home with them was going to invite a lot of awkward questions, questions that for the time being they might be reluctant to answer.

"Best to keep the whole thing quiet until we know a little more about where we stand," mused Nev quietly. "Make careful note of our position and come back another day. No-one else is likely to stumble across it."

Barney got up to enter the cabin and retrieved the chart. He returned looking mystified as he laid it on the cockpit table. "No mention of a wreck here. And, according to the figures, we're also in seventy feet of water. No mention of a reef either."

Nev rubbed his stubbly chin as he too stared at the chart. "It must have been the reef that holed the brig. Then she must have slipped right down the murky depths to one side. Did ye see... the other thing?"

Barney looked at him intensely, studying his face for clues. "Yes. What the hell was it? It looked like another boat – but one that could have sailed straight out of St Tropez or Key West just last week."

"That's just what it was. *Seaspray*. I saw the name on the side. And there's something else...."

Barney felt the hairs on the back of his neck rise as he waited for his friend to finish his sentence.

"...I saw two skeletons, trapped in their seats by debris."

Now they faced a moral dilemma. Their clear duty was to report the find for the sake of grieving relatives who probably had no idea of *Seaspray*'s fate. The bodies – what was left of them – could then be recovered for proper burial.

But that would mean revealing their other discovery to the entire world.

"We're going to have to think very seriously about this," murmured Nev quietly, almost to himself.

So – like those of mice and men – their great plan was abridged, the expedition severely edited. Barney and Nev decided to press on to Lanai, so as to not make any suspiciously sudden changes, but they would hole up there for a day or two and mull things over.

They were uncharacteristically quiet as they headed for the next island, the telescope wrapped in protective towelling and carefully stowed with the fishing gear. Barney and Nev had been searched once by the coastguard during a clampdown on the inter-island narcotics trade, but it had been only a cursory check. The smiling officers hadn't even looked for dummy fuel tanks built into the Buccaneer or anything serious like that. Both men knew that the boat would have been far more vigorously torn apart had there been any real suspicions. It had been just a routine check – everyone knew Barney and Ben, The Underwater Men!

Besides, the coastguard crew had left their jackets off – a sure sign they weren't taking this particular search very seriously.

So, there was a risk, but a small one. They would take the telescope with them at least as far as Lanai.

It was dusk as they sailed into the harbour and 'Cheesecake Charlie' – as the harbourmaster was known – gave them a cheerful shout, lifting his battered straw hat and waving his arms to assure them there was plenty of space for their little 30-footer.

You couldn't miss Charlie – his shirt was so loud you could have shoved him in a lighthouse and used him as a foghorn. Such flowery shirts are de rigeur in the islands.

As the light faded, Barney and Nev busied themselves with securing the Buccaneer for the night. Suddenly Nev's voice boomed uncharacteristically curt from the cockpit while Barney was making fast the mooring ropes.

"Ok wee funny guy, where is it?" yelled Nev.

Barney didn't catch on.

"Where's what?"

"The bleedin' telescope, that's what – the towel's here but the scope's GONE. Where the hell have you hidden it?"

Barney was confused. He knew his friend was serious. "Don't be a jester – I haven't touched it since you put it there."

"Well, it's not there now. So ye must have moved it. Now don't be a complete prat – *where is it*?"

Barney hopped back into the cockpit and strode over to where Nev was desperately scrabbling through the fishing gear.

"Nev, for Chrissakes, I haven't touched it. It *must* be there."

Eventually, both men stopped their fruitless searching and stood staring at each other, Nev aggressive and Barney slightly defensive. Then, with an indecipherable grunt Nev stormed out of the cockpit and jumped up onto the quayside to head for Juicy Lucy's. "For God's sake," he mumbled as he strode over the wooden boards.

Barney scratched his head, considered one more thorough look over the boat and then, in desperation, turned to follow Nev.

Later the two men squared up in Juicy Lucy's makeshift bar. Barney knew there was big trouble brewing because up in their room Nev had been humming the ominous harmony of the Black Bear as he shaved. The Black Bear is a notoriously aggressive reel designed to fire the Scottish heart. When Nev started humming it, he was usually drunk, with the furies on his brain. Best to stay well clear.

"I don't know what to say," Barney began. "It's just a complete mystery. One minute it was there – the next, gone."

"It's gone alright," said Nev abruptly, quaffing down a giant gulp of his favourite malt. Barney could see the Black Bear was still pounding in his brain.

"Nev... you can't possibly think I've taken it," his tone was imploring. "For God's sake, there's enough jam and honey down there to keep us both going 'til Judgement Day! Why would I try and steal the telescope?"

Nev was silent. He considered Barney's words, but obviously remained unconvinced.

They stayed at Juicy Lucy's for two more nights and the atmosphere remained tense. They searched the boat again, together and individually, but found nothing but the slightly-greened towelling, the only indication the telescope had ever been hidden there.

Finally Nev said it for both of them.

“I’m taking the inter-island shuttle back to Oahu – you do what you like with the boat,” he snapped. Barney didn’t know what to say, so he didn’t say anything. Sadly but silently he watched his friend pack a few things together before taking a cab to the tiny airstrip.

His last words as Nev climbed into the back of the battered old Chevrolet taxi were: “Nev, I didn’t take it.”

His friend didn’t reply. He slammed the door shut and the car rumbled off in a cloud of grit. Barney was left standing by the side of the dusty road, staring after him. Confused and feeling somehow betrayed.

Barney decided to nurse his grievances in his time-honoured way, alone with the ocean, and continued the scheduled journey around the islands as planned. It wasn’t so much fun solo but it cleared his head a little. He badly missed his Scottish friend’s often acid banter.

But by the time he returned to Waikiki several days later he was faced with another shock. Nevis had upped and left the beach house, taking all his things with him. It was typical of him. No note, no explanation, not a word. He was just gone.

Probably still humming the Black Bear.

Apart from living on their own, life continued much as before. They were still business partners and they both turned up every day at the beach ‘office’ – a not very converted boathouse. They talked, nominally, but whenever Barney tried to broach the subject of the telescope Nev just turned cold as stone.

Barney would have given up, but – just like any couple who had been living together – there were complications. Quite apart from the joint ownership of the house there still lurked the dark dilemma of *Seaspray*, found bizarrely cradled on the deck of the sunken galleon.

“We’ve got to decide what to do about those bodies, Nev,” said Barney after two full weeks had gone by. “I’ve checked with maritime records and it went missing two years ago. Despite a massive investigation they never found a thing. The search was abandoned after a month.”

“Aye, I ken,” muttered Nev. “Jack Stevenson and his nephew Adrian Sharpe.” Nev had obviously done his own research. “They put it down to some sort of freak storm.”

"Well?" said Barney impatiently. "We've got to tell the authorities. The families are still grieving because they don't have any bodies to bury."

"The sea buries its own," mumbled Nev. "But, aye, you're right. First, I propose we go back there to take another look. Maybe grab a little more treasure before we throw in the towel."

"Yeah, why not," agreed Barney, relieved to see a little of the old twinkle back in his pal's eye. The old team was back together and the game was on.

The next day the Buccaneer was over the reef and the friends toppled one after the other over the side. Just as before, the sea was as clear and blue as only the Pacific can be and both men marvelled that neither wreck had been spotted from the air.

This time they had an unexpected scare – two six-foot sharks suddenly appeared from the bowels of the man-o-war, but even as their hearts lurched, both men realized these were harmless white-tips. Nothing more or less than sleek, subterranean, bio-engineered perfection.

Satisfied there was nothing more menacing waiting for him below decks, Nevis did his usual vanishing trick while Barney waited and kept watch outside. A few minutes later Nev reappeared, this time clutching two coral-encrusted finds both looking like modern sculptures.

A short while later, on the deck of the Buccaneer, Barney hid a strange feeling as he watched his friend carefully work at the barnacled surfaces. He didn't know it, but Nev was sharing exactly the same misgivings.

"Either I'm a Dutchman or this long piece looks precisely like the telescope that we dinna mention," he said brightly. Before long both items were uncovered and laying side by side on the bench. One was an extremely ornate chalice about nine inches high with definite traces of gold, silver and perhaps other gems. Priceless, declared Nev.

The other was a telescope – *the* telescope? – the exact twin of the one they had found before.

"Bugger me bagpipes," intoned Nev, and added a long, low whistle just for effect. "So that's what ye did, ye little rascal, ye covered it all up with barnacles and plopped it back in the sea for me to find all over again."

But behind the joking, both men were so baffled they were petrified. “There just couldn’t be two of them exactly the same,” said Barney, visibly shaking. “There just couldn’t.”

They studied it from this angle and that, and the more they probed the more they were convinced it *was* the same telescope.

There could, unfortunate though it was for each man’s personal sanity, be no doubt.

“What the hell is going on?” asked Barney lamely. “I’ve never known a telescope that thinks it’s a bloody boomerang.”

“I’ve nay idea at all,” responded Nev. “But I suggest we get back down there and grab a few more things before we have to go and dump this in someone else’s lap.”

They agreed, nothing too ostentatious, nothing too big; just a souvenir or two to keep them warm in their old age. Then they could let someone else worry about the murky mystery of it all. So an hour or two later they had compiled a veritable treasure trove in the cabin of the Buccaneer. Gold necklaces, earrings, coins of all ages and denominations, flamboyantly decorated cups, dishes and chalices. They ignored the larger guns – including of course, cannon – but had ‘rescued’ several ancient small-arms, swords and jewel-encrusted knives.

The whole lot they reckoned conservatively to be worth at least half a million pounds sterling.

“OK, let’s get the blazes out of here,” said Nev and they scrambled to hide everything from prying eyes as best they could before starting the Buccaneer’s engine.

The familiar purr of the three-litre Evinrude was like music to their ears as they pulled away towards Oahu. Except – they didn’t.

“What theeeeeeeee?” screamed Barney as he distinctly felt the Buccaneer actually sliding backwards. “Something’s pulling us back!”

“We’re going under!” yelled Nev as the Buccaneer’s engine raced to a high-pitched whine, struggling against the reverse pull. Desperately both men stared over the side and saw for themselves that the whole boat was being *sucked* under the waves.

The normal three feet of white infrastructure above the water was fast being reduced to two feet... one foot... six inches. Any second and the rear cockpit would flood as the ocean poured over the rim. The engine was powerless to resist. The whole vessel was being pulled inexorably into the ocean from the stern.

"The gold..." spluttered Nev, and Barney was astounded to see him race forward into the cabin as if to save their treasures. But as he emerged with a handful of relics and began to throw them overboard, Barney caught on. He too ducked inside and pulled out as much as he could by the armful. Both men were tipping the wealth of their dreams back into the ocean like so much unwanted fish.

Finally it was all done and the small boat was released from the grip of the unseen force that had threatened to drag it down to the depths to join the sunken galleon. The engine once more took control, with a lurch that threw them sprawling onto the deck. They scrambled to their feet and watched the broiling waters behind them as they sped towards home.

"What the hell was that?" said Barney.

"I reckon we had something someone wanted back, badly." replied Barney.

"You mean...?"

"Search me," Nev went on. "All I know is what we saw. As soon as the relics were back where they came from we were... freed."

"Freed?" said Barney as he steered for home with the throttle as far out as it would go.

"What would you call it?"

"Freed," Barney considered the feel of the word with his tongue. "I guess we now know what happened to *Seaspray.*"

"Only they obviously didn't think to give it back."

"Jesus Christ, this can't be real," said Barney. "This can't have happened."

Nev was still staring back at the patch of ocean now far behind, its waters no longer disturbed. "Tell that to *Seaspray,*" he said quietly. "Tell that to *Seaspray.*"

There is a postscript to this story. Nev and Barney never actually got married, but they stayed together a few years after these bizarre events, still sharing the Waikiki beach-house and generally bickering, boozing and partying their lives away. Some folks on the islands said they drank like men who had something pretty serious to forget.

They discovered when they returned to Oahu that they had overlooked one tiny gold ring in the cabin of the Buccaneer. They kept a close watch on it, waiting hour by hour for it to suddenly 'vanish', just as the telescope had mysteriously done.

When 24 hours had passed and the ring was still there, Nev sent it special delivery to a pal of his at LA university, Trevor Wallace, who held an impressive doctorate in relics and antiquities.

A short time after that, Trevor was talking anxiously to Nev on the phone, an extremely late night call.

"You're not going to believe this, Ben..."

"It's vanished. Disappeared," said Nev coolly.

"How the hell did you know?" demanded Trevor. "It was there, right there... in my locker. Completely safe. But when I checked on it this evening..."

"Gone," interjected Nev. "Like the wind. Whoosh!"

"Ben, I hope you don't think..."

But Nev was ahead of him. "Don't worry about it. It probably had to fly."

"What?"

"Never mind."

"Ben, I just can't believe it. The thing was at least 300 years old and worth a certain $5,000 on the open market. But, believe me, nobody could have stolen it. My university office locker was still securely locked."

"Dinna ye worry about it," said Nev consolingly. "Thanks anyway." And he hung up the phone.

The next day was more embarrassing when the pals told the coastguard about the wreck and the *Seaspray* skeletons, carefully omitting several vaguely controversial details.

They returned to the spot with them and two island detectives. But the galleon and *Seaspray* were nowhere to be seen. Even the reef was gone. They were just sitting over 70 feet of empty ocean.

"I hope this isn't some kind of sick joke," warned the more surly-looking of the policemen.

Later the boys paid a visit to Alice Sharpe, the mother of one of *Seaspray*'s victims, in an attempt to calm the troubled waters they themselves had muddied.

"I've always thought there was something extremely odd about all this," she said kindly, having listened to their heavily edited version of events.

"Don't worry – I have no doubt that you fellahs did see *Seaspray* and the bodies – and acted in everyone's best interests..."

Barney and Nev shuffled a tad uncomfortably at this, but their polite, fixed smiles never faltered as they sipped the old lady's coffee from her best china.

"...You know there was a rumour in the family that Adrian and his uncle had found some sunken wreck somewhere, laden with treasure. They kept it to themselves and were always going out on mysterious trips in my brother's boat but nobody ever really believed the stories hinted at by Adrian. It's not as if they ever brought any treasure home or anything. Adrian was only seventeen, and an imaginative boy."

The two friends bade their farewells to Adrian's very understanding mother and decided it was time to go back to their less complex lives on the beach.

There was something distinctly comforting in being known simply as Barney and Ben, the Underwater Men.

~~ The End ~~

More from Stephen Atkinson

Editor Kay Green writes: most Circaidy Gregory books are by authors who have appeared in the shortlists of Earlyworks Press competitions. The competitions are advertised internationally and the standard and range of entries is always good so when the same name appears several times, as Steve's has, I know it's time that author had a book with their name on the cover.

Steve read *Five Little Pinkies*, one of two of his stories featured in *Ways of Falling*, at the London launch of this prizewinners' anthology in 2010. That cutie of a title disguises a particularly powerful story from the Atkinson oeuvre and is typical of his style – all innocence on the outside, and no clue as to whether you're going to be laughing your socks off or scared to go to bed after the last page.

Ways of Falling pub Earlyworks Press 2010 ISBN 9781906451301 UK£8.99

Steve's haunting tale *Scavenger* first appeared in the anthology Barcelona to Bihar – Steve's story alone takes the reader from a London underpass to the Solomon Islands on a journey never to be forgotten but by the end of the book, there are not many areas of the world which have not featured.

Barcelona to Bihar pub Earlyworks Press 2012 ISBN 9781906451301 UK£8.99

More from Circaidy Gregory Press

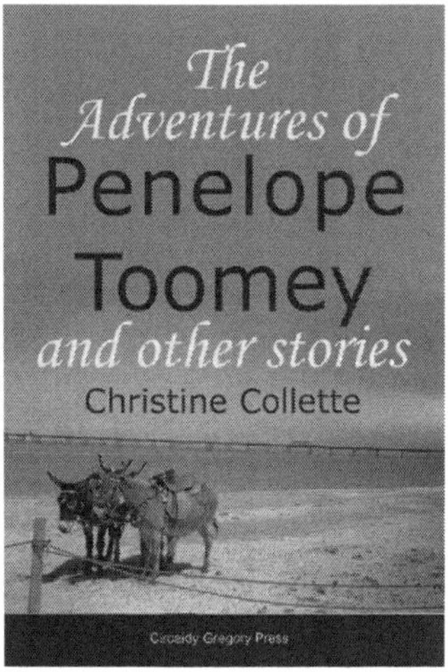

Romance and adventure with laughs, hair-raising dramas and a few tears

Penelope Toomey – Pigs for short – is a heroine with a difference: tubby, debt-ridden and often calamitous. Her adventures range from Paris to Amsterdam, directed by an enigmatic spymaster with whom she falls in love. As well as Penelope's rollercoaster life, this collection brings you a range of stories from both sides of the channel, offering romance with a spice of danger and mystery.

The Adventures of
Penelope Toomey
and other stories

Paperback ISBN 978-1-906451-52-3 £7.99
Also available as an ebook

Small Poisons

Catherine Edmunds

A contemporary novel for Midsummer Night's Dreamers

With charm, wit and magical style, Catherine Edmunds conjures a fairy tale for grown-ups, a fantasy with its feet firmly on the ground, in a place where dreams and stark reality meet. *- Neil Marr*

I promise you, you will never look at your garden the same way again...
– *John Irvine*

I haven't read it yet because my dad saw it and wanted to read it. He was impressed. – *Keith, Texas*

Loved the book. So did my landlady!
– *Mark, London*

Paperback ISBN 978-1-906451-16-5
£9.50 Also available as an ebook

www.circaidygregory.co.uk